PLAIN JANE
MARRIES THE BOSS

Elizabeth Harbison

ROMANCE™

Published by Silhouette Books

America's Publisher of Contemporary Romance

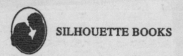

SILHOUETTE BOOKS

RECYCLED PAPER

ISBN 0-373-19416-1

PLAIN JANE MARRIES THE BOSS

Copyright © 1999 by Elizabeth Harbison

Visit us at www.romance.net

Printed in U.S.A.

Books by Elizabeth Harbison

Silhouette Romance

A Groom for Maggie #1239
Wife Without a Past #1258
Two Brothers and a Bride #1286
True Love Ranch #1323
*Emma and the Earl #1410
*Plain Jane Marries the Boss #1416

*Cinderella Brides

ELIZABETH HARBISON

has been an avid reader for as long as she can remember. After devouring the Nancy Drew and Trixie Beldon series in grade school, she moved on to the suspense of Mary Stewart, Dorothy Eden and Daphne du Maurier, just to name a few. From there it was a natural progression to writing, although early efforts have been securely hidden away in the back of a closet.

After authoring three cookbooks, Elizabeth turned her hand to writing romances and hasn't looked back. Her second book for Silhouette Romance, *Wife Without a Past*, was a 1998 finalist for the Romance Writers of America's prestigious RITA Award in the Best Traditional Romance category.

Elizabeth lives in Maryland with her husband, John, and daughter, Mary Paige, as well as two dogs, Bailey and Zuzu. She loves to hear from readers and you can write to her c/o Box 1636, Germantown, MD 20875.

MARRIAGE CONTRACT
BETWEEN TERRENCE BRECKENRIDGE III
AND JANE MILLER

1. Both parties should ignore the sparks that ignite between them whenever they are in a room together. (Remember, you are just colleagues trying to save Mr. Breckenridge's company.)

2. Both shall forget the soul-touching kisses they have already exchanged and never engage in such activities again.

3. If, after all this, either party falls in love with the other signatory to this contract...well, that is *their* problem and this office shall not be held responsible in any way.

Signed: _Terrence Breckenridge III_
Terrence Breckenridge III

Signed: _Jane Miller_
Jane Miller

Chapter One

He entered the office humming. Humming! After all the stress he'd been under in the past couple of months, the pensive silences and long hours burning the midnight oil? Jane Miller couldn't have been more surprised if her boss had carried a lamp post to swing himself around.

"Tonight's the night, Jane." He smiled broadly. She loved his teeth. Even, white teeth, made more charming by a slight crookedness in his smile.

In his French-tailored charcoal-gray suit, which Jane had noticed long ago picked up a light in his gray eyes and made his glossy dark hair look as black as pitch, he looked every inch the distinguished executive. Terrence Breckenridge III. Not many people were regal enough to carry such a name, but it fit Trey like a fine leather glove.

Most of the people in the offices of Breckenridge

Construction said he should be a movie star. Jane agreed that he had the looks and the charisma to draw millions of fans, but she also knew he would never be interested in that sort of fame. Fortune, yes, but fame, no. He was too private for that. It was one of the things that attracted her the most about him during the five years she'd worked as his administrative assistant.

"Tonight's the night," he said again, and reached down to pull her out of her chair, whirling her around in what was probably a good imitation of Fred Astaire dancing with a coat rack.

"I—I have an important message for you," Jane said stiffly, fixing her glasses and trying to regain her balance. Truthfully, though, her wobbly knees had more to do with his proximity than the fact that he was whirling her around the floor like a top.

"A message." He pulled her close, as if to begin a tango. He smelled wonderful, she noticed—clean as spring but with a vague hint of sultry autumn—and the warmth of his body aligned with hers made her dizzy with excitement. "What's the message?" he asked dramatically. He was joking with her but his mouth was so close to her ear that his low voice sent tremors down her spine.

She pulled away gracelessly, afraid that if she didn't get some distance quickly she might try to get closer and make a real fool of herself. "One if by land, two if by sea," she said with a smile, but her voice was thin with nerves. She smoothed back strands of her long auburn hair which had come loose from the heavy braid she wore down her back.

He clicked his tongue against his teeth. "Really, Jane, you're going to have to start getting my messages to me sooner. That one's already in the history books." He smiled again and cocked his head toward his office. "Come on in, and have some coffee."

She took a steno pad and pen off her desk. "As long as I bring it myself with a cup for you too, right?"

"Isn't that part of a secretary's job?"

"Administrative assistant."

He lifted an eyebrow persuasively. "Girl friday?"

"Administrative assistant," she said again, but she couldn't help smiling.

"Ah." He nodded. "In that case, can I get you a cup of coffee?" He started toward the machine across the room. "How do you take it? Just cream?"

A flush of pleasure washed over her. He knew how she liked her coffee. That tiny fact made her feel almost giddy. Immediately, she pushed the feeling away, remembering what she had to tell him. She glanced at her desk, at the *While You Were Out...* message pad. Dread niggled in the back of her mind. She wasn't sure how he'd feel about this.

As well as she knew him, as thoroughly as she could predict his reactions in business, she had never been able to figure out his emotions or private life. Heaven knew she'd tried.

He was humming again. She hated to stop him, but there was no time to waste.

"Trey, seriously, I have a message for you." She swallowed. "From Victoria."

He stopped and was very still. Without turning

around, he said, "Don't tell me she's canceling," in a tone that suggested this would be a major calamity.

Jane fought the disappointment she felt at the fact that he cared so much. Thanks to the sheen of nervous perspiration on her face, her glasses slipped down the bridge of her nose and she pushed them back hastily.

He turned to face her and she knew she must be a terrible sight compared with the mental picture of Victoria he undoubtedly had right now. "Look, Trey, why don't we go into your office so I can explain?"

"Tell me she's not canceling on me tonight," he repeated, the blood draining from his handsome face in an almost cartoon-like fashion.

Her heart beat a furious rhythm. She couldn't believe she had to say this to him. She heaved a shuddering breath. Five years. For five years, nearly six, she'd wanted nothing more than to be with Trey, romantically. Not only had that not even come close to happening, but now she had to *break up with him for someone else!* "I'm afraid it's worse than that." She drew in a breath and let it out slowly. *Just say it,* she told herself. *Get it over with.* "She's...she's getting married."

Trey stared at her in apparent disbelief.

"To someone else," Jane added, unnecessarily.

"What, tonight?" Trey said at last. His tone was steeped in incredulity. "She's getting married *tonight?*"

"Yes." Jane took a steadying breath. Trey and Victoria had been going out together for exactly six months, one week and three days. Surely he had had an idea that there was someone else in Victoria's life. "She said to tell you that someone named Bill had finally asked her and she wasn't taking any chances by waiting and letting him change his mind."

He raked a hand through his hair. "She's waited three years for this guy—couldn't she wait one more night?"

"You know about him?"

"Of course. Bill Lindon from Cosbot Technologies. Very big fish in a big ocean." He gave a dry laugh. "She'll make a good socialite." His face darkened. "Which was exactly what I wanted her to do tonight."

Jane's heart, which had been pounding furiously, suddenly seemed to stop. "What do you mean? You're not upset that she's getting married, just that she's doing it *tonight?*" Her heart rose. That she should feel hopeful at the idea that he didn't love Victoria was as silly as a teenager being hopeful that a rock star was available. But she was hopeful nevertheless.

"Why should I be upset that she's getting married?"

Jane frowned. "Because she's your...aren't you two..." She took a breath. "I just thought you two were an item."

His expression lifted momentarily. "An item?" He gave a laugh. "I don't think either one of us has time for that sort of thing." He hesitated. "At least, I don't."

"Then you're not involved?" The words came out

in a rush and she instantly regretted being so transparent.

He looked at her with a puzzled expression on his face. "No. She was an actress, trying to get herself known in the same circles I have to socialize with now and then. We just went out together sometimes when the occasion called for couples. Served us both well, although she's benefitting more than I am at the moment."

Jane couldn't help smiling broadly. He was free. Her pulse raced. There was no woman in his life at all. "Then don't you find it romantic that she's running off to get married?"

Trey gave a derisive snort. "Romantic for her, maybe, but damned inconvenient for me."

"I don't understand."

"I was planning on taking her to dinner tonight. I was counting on it. What am I going to do now?" He turned to walk toward his office, dazed.

Jane followed at a careful distance. As well as she knew him, she didn't understand this reaction at all. "Couldn't you take someone else to dinner instead?"

He turned and looked at her with a helpless expression that she'd never seen on his face before. "Where am I going to find someone to say she'll marry me at the last minute?" He walked to his desk and flopped into his mahogany leather chair looking so much like a discouraged child that Jane felt the urge to wrap her arms around him.

"Marry you," she said in a rush of breath. She sat down opposite him and tried to keep her face from showing the devastation—not to mention confusion—she felt inside. "I don't get it. You were planning on marrying Victoria?"

He looked at her blankly. "I wasn't really going to marry her."

"But you just said…"

"Nah, we were just going to say that." He tipped the *Ocean in a Box* on his desk and watched the waves swell left and right. "I just needed to create that illusion. Just for tonight."

Jane pinched the bridge of her nose to ward off a rapidly impending headache. "Why?"

"My father is in town briefly and I think he's ready to sign over his shares of the company to me, *if* he believes I'm settling down into family life. When he does," he held his arms out expansively, "I will finally have a controlling interest in this company."

"You ought to," Jane agreed. Trey had taken Breckenridge Construction from being a small-time contractor to being the most prestigious construction and building renovation company in Dallas. Maybe even in all of Texas. "But is it really all that urgent for you to hold control of the company? It's just on paper, after all."

"That's the point. It's not just on paper. If my father keeps putting the kibosh on jobs he doesn't approve of, you know what we'll be?"

"No, what?"

"The biggest school playground builders in Dallas. That is, until we go broke. Which wouldn't take long."

"But we've got the Davenport contract. That's worth millions."

"Exactly." Trey jabbed a finger in the air. "If my father gets wind of that contract he'll vote it down in a heartbeat."

"He doesn't know about it?"

Trey gave a dry laugh. "No way. The Davenport hotel chain was started by a man who was a staunch supporter of a political candidate my father couldn't stand."

"Does that matter?"

"It shouldn't. But my father and Gutterson nearly came to blows over politics twice that I can remember. For twenty-five years now my father has refused to have anything to do with the company, even though Gutterson himself is long gone."

"I see."

"So we're walking a tightrope. My father's here for three days, during which time he has to not hear about the Davenport contract *and* sign the controlling shares of the company over to me."

Jane nodded. "But I don't quite understand what being a family man has to do with running the company."

She was almost sure his expression softened when he looked at her. "Neither do I, but those are his conditions. He's always had this weird thing about wanting me to settle down and, as he says, get my priorities straight before taking on the whole company."

She didn't think that was so weird, but decided it would be best if she didn't say so.

"So I sort of led him to believe that I was in a serious relationship, headed straight for the altar." He absently touched the ring finger on his left hand.

"Ah, I see." Finally she was beginning to understand. Victoria was an actress. She wasn't really Trey's girlfriend, but she played the role as part of an agreement between them. In a strange sort of way it made sense. It certainly explained why they had so often asked Jane to get Victoria on the phone at the last minute when an event came up. It also explained why he usually had Jane arrange for a car to pick Victoria up and take her wherever it was they were going, rather than picking her up himself.

How ironic that Trey had asked someone else to play the role of girlfriend for him when Jane wanted the job so desperately herself. But he couldn't see that. And she couldn't show it.

"Don't look at me like that."

"Like what?" she asked, instinctively raising a hand to her face.

"Like I'm the devil himself."

"I wasn't."

"You know, I do have the company's best interest at heart here." He shrugged. "It was a harmless lie, good for my father, good for me and good for the company."

"Everyone wins?"

"Exactly. You do realize that if we keep going the way we are, with no solid leadership, we're going to have to do some downsizing? That means people will lose their jobs. I could prevent that, if I had control."

"Can't you just buy more shares yourself?"

He shook his head. "I've done everything I could to get more shares, and our other investors, at least the ones I can identify, just aren't budging."

Jane began to calculate the worth of her own shares, then stopped. It wasn't even close to what he would need. She was saving for her eventual retirement, so her interest was based on the forty-year savings plan, not controlling shares. "But if your father is willing to sign over his shares—"

"That's just it. If he's willing. But now..." He made a gesture of futility. "Unless Victoria shows up, he's going to go back to Europe and leave me here with my piddly eighteen percent. I mean, telling him I'm serious about a relationship and then losing the girl looks worse than never having been serious in the first place."

"I see."

"Though it wouldn't necessarily have to be Victoria..." He tapped his fingers on the desk. "It could be anyone."

Jane's mouth suddenly felt dry. "Doesn't your father know who Victoria is?"

He shrugged. "Actually, no. I never said her name. He lives in Tuscany—"

"The south of France," Jane corrected automatically, still thinking about the fact that Victoria wasn't really a contender after all.

"What's that?"

She returned her attention to the conversation. "It's the south of France, not Tuscany." She'd heard the stories of how the elder Terrence Breckenridge had suddenly abandoned the business he'd founded to move to a quiet life near Provence. It was Jane's fantasy that someday she, too, would have that kind of nerve, so his destination had stuck in her mind.

"South of France, that's right." Trey looked impressed. "When we spoke, it was a bad phone connection, I just told him we'd talk about it when he got here." Optimism was lighting his eyes. "And now that he's here, I need a girl. Fast."

Jane sensed disaster in that plan. "Can't you just tell your father the truth?"

"No way." He gave a spike of humorless laughter and leaned back in his chair. "This is harmless enough and—you're looking at me that way again. What's wrong?"

She shook her head. "It's none of my business."

"But?"

She shrugged. How could she tell him all the things that were running through her mind, about him and marriage and love? "I just take the idea of marriage seriously."

"So do I. That's why I don't want anything to do with it." He leaned forward. "I have a theory that nothing kills all hope for future happiness like getting married."

Her heart sank. "That's a depressing thought."

"I know it is, but it's true. I don't know of one lasting union that's turned out happy." He paused. "Do you?"

"Many," she answered quickly. Immediately she questioned herself. Could she say her parents? Her father had died when she was eleven, but until then they had seemed happy together. Her mother had certainly been unhappy once he was gone.

"Name one."

"I could name several, but no one you know."

"Hmm." He obviously didn't believe her.

"Can't you think of even one?"

"Not one."

"How about your parents?" It was a mistake, she realized immediately.

Trey's expression froze. His mouth was still turned up in the suggestion of a smile but the humor had left his eyes. "In my opinion, marriage is an institution that doesn't work."

Very bad subject. She made a mental note of it. "Okay, so does your father know you feel that way about marriage?"

He shook his head. "Nope. Unfortunately, I've got to play his little game if I want to win."

"All to get the company?"

His eyes hardened. "I've worked damn hard to build this business, and if you get right down to it, the old man's not exactly playing fair by ransoming it for a promise of marriage."

"Do you really feel marriage is such a bad thing?" She gathered her courage. "Or do you think you just haven't met the right girl yet?"

He considered her for a moment. "Let me put it this way, my relationship with you is the longest relationship I've ever had with a woman." He gave a half smile. "I don't think that's going to change. But if I create the impression that I'm involved and heading toward the altar to make the old man happy, it's not so bad, is it?''

"I guess not." But she wasn't sure.

He straightened up. "Then you understand."

"I think I do." She wasn't sure at all.

He heaved a breath. "Victoria was perfect for the job."

Meaning, Jane supposed, that not only was she an actress, but she was gorgeous. Looks were almost all that were required. She looked down, privately wishing, for the thousandth time, that she could have just a week of being perfect in the way that blond, petite curvaceous Victoria Benson was. Just to see what it felt like.

At five feet eleven and skinny as a rail, Jane had always felt awkward and conspicuous. Some people might have reveled in that, but she was also so painfully shy that the fact that her height called so much attention to her was the cruelest irony.

So for most of her twenty-six years she'd tried to blend in, to be as unnoticeable as possible. She kept her straight hair pulled back, wore plain black-rimmed glasses, neutral functional clothes and no makeup. It worked. People hardly noticed her, especially if she wasn't right next to them.

She was, in the most literal sense, a plain Jane. The old-fashioned name which had been her grandmother's suited her well.

Across from her, Trey cocked his head and looked at her intensely. "Jane, you wouldn't..."

She frowned. "Wouldn't what?"

He leaned forward in what she recognized as his

pitch position. "Jane, you know I'd never want you to do something you're uncomfortable with."

Her heart lurched to her throat. "Like making coffee for my boss?" She tried to make her tone light but her voice was barely more than a whisper.

He smiled. "How about pretending you're engaged to your boss?"

Had she heard him correctly? Or had she slipped into a dream? "You want *me* to—"

"You're right, it's completely outside the bounds of your job description. I have no right to even ask, but I'm asking anyway. Will you even consider it?"

Jane felt the heat of self-consciousness creep into her cheeks. "Trey, who would believe you'd marry me?"

"Why not?" He looked genuinely puzzled and for that she felt more affection for him than she ever had before.

Her chest warmed into an ache. "Well, I'm hardly a glamour girl."

He leaned back in his chair and appraised her. "I don't even know what that means. You'd do just fine." He must have realized how unenthusiastic that sounded because he immediately added, "You'd be great. Probably even better than Victoria."

Jane gave a laugh. "There's no way you're going to make me believe that."

"Please consider it," he said soberly. "Please."

"It would never work."

"It has to."

She took a slow, calming breath. "Well…"

"Is that a yes?"

"If you really think this can work…"

"Is that a yes?" he pressed again. "Please say that's a yes."

She shrugged. "I guess it is."

He smiled broadly. "Jane, Jane, Jane, you are a lifesaver. I don't know how to thank you."

"Just doing my job," she said, in what she had intended to be a joke.

He scoffed. "This goes well beyond the call of duty. Obviously I'll pay you overtime for this."

"Pay?" she echoed in a whisper. "I was only kidding. You wouldn't need to pay me."

"Of course I would, it's work. I'll give you time and a half. No, double time."

"That's really not necessary. I'm honestly glad to be able to help."

He gave a long sigh that was clearly relief, and looked at her with unabashed pleasure. "There aren't a lot of girls like you in this world."

She raised an eyebrow and started to speak, but he interrupted her. "Women," he corrected. "People. There aren't a lot of people in the world like you."

She smiled. "Or like you."

His smile dimmed fractionally and he looked at her with serious eyes. "What on earth would I ever do without you?" The intensity of his gaze, as well as his words, made pleasure coil like a snake in the pit of Jane's stomach.

He appreciated her. She actually meant something to him. Until today she had never really been sure of that.

She glanced down, practically circling her toe on

the ground in front of her. "You'd do fine, Trey. You always do."

Trey watched Jane as she walked away from him. After she closed the door, he slumped down in his chair and let out a long breath. Had he really asked her to play the part of his fiancée tonight? Was he insane?

Maybe she was right. Maybe people wouldn't believe him and Jane as a couple. They were so different from each other. He saw the big picture not the details. He tended to create a lot of clutter in his quest to achieve his goals. Jane, on the other hand, was practical and no-nonsense. She was incredibly efficient, and always behaved in a prim and proper manner. In her own way, he realized, Jane was no more the marrying kind than he was.

Which, actually, made her perfect for him.

He blew air into his cheeks, then sighed it away. Jane. She wasn't always prim and proper. In fact, there were aspects of her that were undeniably... sexy. For example, there was the subtle sway of her slender hips as she'd walked away. He hadn't been able to ignore that. Of course, it had caught his eye because he rarely saw a woman who wasn't consciously doing it and he knew Jane wasn't. It was interesting, that was all. It wasn't really what you would call lust or anything.

He rubbed his eyes and tried to shake the thought out of his head. Jane would be horrified if she had any idea he was thinking this way. She'd probably even quit. He could picture it now, Jane sitting before him, in her high-necked blouse, hands folded in her lap.

I'm sorry, Trey, but I'm unable to work with you under the circumstances. I'm sure you'll understand why I feel... What would she say? Probably something delicate and old-fashioned. *I feel we must part.*

He shook his head again. What was he doing, wasting his time thinking about this? He had much more important things to worry about now that the problem of tonight's dinner was patched up.

He looked at the door to make sure it was closed all the way, then took a key ring out of his pocket and opened the side drawer of his desk. What he needed was right on top. It was a composition notebook he'd picked up at the drug store for a buck. Something about the informality of the book was comforting to him, like its contents weren't necessarily serious.

He opened to the first page and it hit him full force. The contents were serious all right. It was a list of employees' names, beginning with those who were most expendable, if such a word could really be used for people. He trailed his finger down the list looking for... For what? For young, single, independently wealthy people whose lives wouldn't be devastated by the loss of their job? There weren't any. Most of the names were familiar. Good, reliable, loyal workers who had worked for the company for over ten years. He'd hate to lay any of them off.

After several long minutes, he put the composition book back and took out the spreadsheet his accountant had done. There was a dip in November two years ago, right about the time Trey's father had voted against bidding on a job for a company he felt was too commercial. He said the company "didn't nurture the community spirit that Breckenridge Construction had built its good name upon."

That had been Trey's first real clash with his father. Up to that point, they had lived in peaceful estrangement. They were acquaintances, little more. All that changed that November, though. Trey had first tried reasoning with his father, pointing out that the company had to grow in order to justify retaining the existing employees. That had been met with blame for "overspending" by "overemploying." So Trey had changed his tactic, insisting that limiting the company that way would endanger its very existence.

He believed the word his father had responded with was, "Hogwash."

Finally Trey had demanded that they go forward with the bid. His father had called an emergency Board meeting and vote. His shares had easily won the vote, as he knew they would.

Trey looked back at the spreadsheet and saw where something similar had happened in February the next year, and May after that. In July his father had finally relented and they'd gotten a semi-large contract for an undeniably commercial health club. The renovation work was up for an award. Trey shook his head. You'd think that would persuade the old man this was the right direction but, no, he was still dragging his feet.

He moved the spreadsheet aside and looked at the

company assets and liabilities. He scanned down the numbers to the bottom of the page. The bottom line. When he saw it, he winced. Breckenridge Construction was in trouble. Big trouble.

If Trey didn't get control of the company in time to take the Davenport job, not only would the people listed in the composition book be without jobs, but most likely Trey, himself, would be too. And Jane. There was no way he could let that happen. He'd do whatever it took to save their jobs for them, and the company for himself.

After all, it was really all he had.

Chapter Two

"This is your chance," Jane told her reflection in the rearview mirror on the way home. "Tonight you're going to be his fiancée. It's up to you to make it real." She looked at her reflection an extra moment, then turned her eyes back to the road with a laugh. "Right. Not unless I have a fairy godmother that I don't know about."

A small, red convertible zipped into the lane in front of Jane, and she had to slam on the brakes of her own sensible American-made compact to avoid a crash. She pulled over to the side of the road and sat, waiting for her pulse to calm down and watching the convertible speed off. All she saw of the driver was long blonde hair flowing in the wind, and a red-nailed hand waving back at Jane.

"Well if that isn't symbolic, I don't know what is," she said to herself and sighed. "I can't keep up in a red convertible world. Why am I trying?"

There wasn't even the lightest of winds to answer. Not that she expected one. She already had more answers than she cared to acknowledge.

"You know darn well what you should do," she said to her reflection again. "You should quit working for Trey and leave. It's the only way to get him out of your system." She pressed her lips together and shook her head, now looking inward instead of at the mirror. "But I can't," she said softly. "I care too much to leave."

After a moment of quiet, she put her car into gear and pulled back onto the road.

As soon as she walked in the front door of her apartment ten minutes later, her roommate, Peatie, shouted to her from the bathroom.

"Your boss called." Peatie's New York accent was uncharacteristically sing-songy. She walked into the hallway, with huge sections of her bleached-blond hair wrapped in aluminum foil. "Said he wasn't sure whether you had something you wanted to wear to this fancy schmancy place tonight, so he's having some things sent over from Neiman-Marcus." She looked at Jane expectantly. "Neiman-Marcus. So what the heck's going on?"

"It's no big deal," Jane said, a flush of anticipation warming her cheeks. She dropped her purse on the hall table and shrugged. "I just have to go out with Trey tonight and pose as his fiancée."

"You *what?*"

"No big deal. All in a day's work." She tried to keep a straight face but when she saw her roommate's astounded expression, she burst into laughter.

Peatie put a hand on her hip. "Okay, okay, you had me going for a minute. Now what are you really up to?"

Jane crossed her finger over her chest. "Honest to goodness, that's what I'm doing. I can't quite believe it either. But Trey wants his father to believe he's engaged, and when the woman who was supposed to play the role canceled, he asked me. Me."

"You're serious?"

Jane nodded. "Unless I'm dreaming."

Peatie frowned, obviously still not convinced. "Why does he want his father to think he's engaged?"

Jane took her sweater off and hung it on the coat rack. "It's a long story, but he's got noble reasons, don't worry."

Peatie shook her foiled head, then gasped. "Oh! He said he wanted you to call him if you got in before five-thirty. You've got like a minute."

Jane glanced at her watch. It was five twenty-five. "Thanks," she said, running to the phone in the kitchen. Was he canceling? No, he wouldn't be sending clothes over if he was. As she rounded the corner, she slipped and her shoe went flying off, but didn't bother retrieving it as she was already reaching for the phone.

Peatie followed Jane, holding the shoe out to her. "Lose something, Cinderella?"

Jane laughed and took the shoe, feeling that the analogy was apt. The phone rang five times, and she was about to hang up when Trey answered.

"Trey, it's Jane," she said in the calmest voice she could manage. "You called?"

"Did your roommate tell you I was having some clothes sent over?" He sounded distracted.

Jane sat down and coiled the phone cord around her finger. "Yes, that's really thoughtful of you, but you didn't have to bother." She was sure glad he had, though, because she hadn't even thought about what to wear.

"It was no bother, but I wanted to make sure you didn't think I was being presumptuous." She could see him setting his pen down and leaning back in his chair in her mind's eye, almost as if he was sitting right in front of her. "It's not that I thought you didn't have clothes already, I just wanted to make sure you didn't feel like you had to run out and get something new. Knowing you, you wouldn't tell me so I could cover the expense."

He was right. She smiled to herself. "It should be interesting to see what you picked out."

His chair squeaked and she knew he was leaning forward again, probably looking at things on his desk and getting ready to hang up the phone. "I picked out a professional shopper. She's picking the clothes. I just hope I got your size right." He sounded distracted again, and she wasn't surprised when he went on to say, "Look, I'm on my way out but I'll see you in a couple of hours, all right?"

He'd see her in a couple of hours. It was almost as if they had a date. "See you then," she said lightly, and hung up the phone.

"So what did the future Mr. Jane Miller have to say?" Peatie asked.

Jane turned to her with a smile. "He wanted to make sure I wasn't offended that he was having clothes sent here."

Peatie snorted. "He can offend me any time he wants to send Neiman's over." An egg timer dinged in the bathroom. "Time to rinse," she said, heading down the hall. "But I want details when I get back."

Jane was about to go to her room when the doorbell buzzed. She hurried to answer.

When she opened the door, a petite woman stood before her holding several heavy-looking garment bags. "Jane Miller?"

"Yes." Jane stepped back to show the woman in.

"I'm Ella Bingham," the woman said, with a warm smile. "Mr. Breckenridge said you'd be expecting me."

"Yes." Jane led her into the living room. "Can I help you carry any of that?"

"Oh, heavens no, thank you. I've spent years doing this sort of thing." She laid the bags across the back of the sofa and stood back to assess Jane. "Let's see now." She walked around her, looking her up and down. "That Mr. Breckenridge has quite a good eye. What do you wear, a twelve?"

Jane was amazed. "Yes. He told you that?"

Ella shook her head. "I don't know a man in the world who's that good. No, he estimated your height and measurements and he did quite well." She winked. "He must spend quite a lot of time with you."

"He's my boss." She wondered why she felt she had to explain.

Ella nodded discreetly and unzipped the first garment bag with a flair. "Mr. Breckenridge wasn't sure what sort of fashion you'd prefer, so I brought a selection." She pulled out a slim red dress with a matching bolero jacket. "He did mention that you remind him of Audrey Hepburn, so I naturally thought of this style."

"It's beautiful," Jane breathed.

Peatie entered the room in a thick terrycloth robe, rubbing her wet hair with a towel. "It sure is. Is that what you're wearing tonight?"

Jane introduced the women, then said, "I don't know..." She looked at Ella, trying to savor every delicious moment of this fantasy evening. "Did Trey really say I reminded him of Audrey Hepburn?"

"He certainly did, and I can see exactly what he meant." Ella gave a demure smile. "Now run along and give this dress a try."

"I don't know..."

"Jane, it's gorgeous," Peatie said.

"Yes, it is, but it's so—so glamorous."

Peatie and Ella exchanged glances and Ella said, "I'll just pop down to the car and get the shoes." She flashed Peatie another look. "See if you can't get her into that dress while I'm gone."

When she was gone, Peatie turned to Jane and asked, "What's the matter?"

"Nothing, it's just...look at that dress and then look at me." She splayed her arms. Did she really have to spell this out? "I'm hardly the model type. I'd look silly in something so…alluring."

Peatie scoffed and dragged Jane by the arm over to the old, brass hallway mirror. "I hate to break this to you, Janie, but you're not quite the monster you make yourself out to be." She wrinkled her nose and studied Jane from her vantage point behind—and about six inches below her. "Actually, I think you'd really be a knockout with a little makeup and hair styling and some different clothes."

Jane flashed her a look.

Peatie laughed. "Look, I'd kill to have your height and your cheekbones."

"Come on, I don't believe that for a minute."

"I mean it." Peatie gestured emphatically. "Look at yourself. You're Beauty, not the Beast."

Jane's face grew hot as she looked at her reflection. Was Peatie seeing the same thing she was? "All right, I know I'm not a *beast* but at best I'm just ordinary." She moved her gaze from Peatie to her own reflection. "Makeup and clothes aren't going to change me into a beauty."

"How do you know?" Peatie asked derisively. "Honestly, I'll never understand why you always sell yourself so short."

Jane turned to face her roommate, grateful for the compliment but a realist to the end. "I don't sell myself short. I know I have other things going for me. But…" She sighed. "You know, my mother was beautiful. I mean," she gestured at the dress, "that kind of beautiful. I think I was a huge disappointment to her."

"Oh, Jane. Why would you think that?"

Jane bit her lower lip and allowed herself a moment to dive into the memories she had avoided for so long. "When I was young, she used to dress me in clothes that matched hers, but as I got older she stopped. She marveled at how *different* I looked from her. Not that she said that was a bad thing, exactly, but I could tell."

"Come on, you're jumping pretty far to reach those conclusions."

Jane gave a quick shake of her head. "It wasn't just that. After my dad died and Mom went to work, she became quite blunt about how I should emphasize my education and not my looks. She said my intelligence was my greatest asset and not to worry about my appearance." She turned back to the mirror and looked at the tall, pale woman she saw there. "I know that's not horrendous, but hearing that from someone who looks like a Hollywood star makes the point pretty obvious."

Peatie clicked her tongue against her teeth. "Well, if you ask me, your mom didn't do you any great favors by making you feel so unfeminine and plain. Especially since it's not true."

Jane sighed. It was awkward to defend either side of this argument. Fortunately, Peatie didn't wait for her to.

"But I can help you with that now," she went on. "Tonight, Cinderella, you're going to the ball. Best of all, your prince is guaranteed."

"This may be the biggest mistake of my life."

Peatie patted Jane's shoulder. "Believe me, this is

a golden opportunity for you. And in that dress," she gave a broad wink, "I bet I won't be seeing you back here again until tomorrow morning."

"Now you're making fun of me."

"I am not!" Peatie looked very serious. "Janie, I would never, ever encourage you to do this if I thought you'd get hurt."

Jane bit down on her lip and glanced at her watch. It was quarter to six. "Okay, I'll try it." She picked the dress up and went down the hallway to her room. Her heart pounded at the idea of actually giving this a try. Maybe—just maybe—it could work. Maybe Trey would finally see her in a romantic light. She began to work up some enthusiasm but a tiny dread nagged in her chest. She stopped and turned back. "Peatie, what if I make a fool of myself?"

Peatie shrugged. "What of it? Will you feel worse if you make a fool of yourself trying to get this guy or if you never even try at all?"

"I don't know." Her palms were cold and wet. "I honestly don't know the answer to that question."

"Yes, you do." Peatie smiled in a knowing way. Then her voice became crisp and businesslike as she cracked an imaginary whip. "Now try on that dress."

As she walked through the doors of the Zebra Room, Jane clutched her serviceable black, wool coat closed around her and tried hard to keep believing.

It wasn't always easy.

But she tried. Peatie and Ella's enthusiasm had been infectious and she'd left the house in the fire-engine red dress, which, as it turned out, hugged her figure in all the right places, and made her look more lithe and elegant than she'd ever dreamed she could.

"You can't tell what something's going to look like until you take it off the rack and try it on," Ella had said. "The dress doesn't make you stunning, it's the other way around."

"I don't know," Jane had answered, still breathless from the dramatic enhancement she'd seen in the mirror. "I still think this is some sort of miracle dress."

"It's a few yards of fabric," Peatie had said, and Ella nodded. "What you're looking at is you."

Jane had smiled at that. Perhaps it was true. Somehow she felt more like herself than she ever had before, even though she had thought it would be the opposite. She felt proud and confident, or at least as close to confident as she could come, given that she was still Jane. Anyway, she'd left the house—that was progress.

Now every step she took added a spark to her emotionally charged anticipation. It was like wearing tap shoes on a subway line. What would Trey think? Would he see her as the same old plain Jane she'd always been or would he finally see her as the woman she thought maybe—just maybe—she truly was?

Her long auburn hair was curled into Pre-Raphaelite ringlets that tumbled across her shoulders in an unfamiliar way. She'd talked Peatie and Ella out of the red-red lipstick they'd suggested, but the dusty-rose she wore instead felt just as conspicuous.

Plus it made her mouth look huge and pouty. Her lashes, thick and long with black mascara, seemed to stick together for an instant every time she blinked.

And she blinked a lot, because Peatie had insisted she take off her ''sex-prevention glasses'', so everything in the distance had a tendency to blur. Her one small concession to herself was that she'd snuck the glasses into the small clutch bag Ella had thrust upon her.

But in her secret heart, she felt great.

She stopped at the coat check. With one final steadying breath, she took off the coat. A cool breeze drifted through the front door. Her legs, covered in the sheerest silk stockings, felt nude. She congratulated herself for having had the good sense to override Peatie's suggestion that she wear high heels, and instead wore good, solid pumps.

''You can do this,'' she told herself under her breath. ''You can do it.''

''I beg your pardon, madame?'' the maître d' asked, coming away from his station. The older couple in front of her looked miffed at his abandonment. ''Is there some way I can be of service to you?''

It was one of the first times in recent history she hadn't felt invisible in public.

Panic filled her. She wasn't sure what to do with herself. ''I'm just looking for my party. Thank you.'' With the maître d's gaze still burning on her skin, she turned to rush from the restaurant. This was a bad idea. A very bad idea. There was no way in the world she could pull this off. She'd leave a message for Trey, apologizing. Maybe even resigning.

The door was within reach. She could feel the chilly night air on her skin. All she had to do was get her coat and—

Wham! She slammed into something, or rather some*one,* at full force and dropped her purse, spilling the contents across the red, carpeted floor.

Jane dropped to the floor in a frantic scramble to pick the contents up, lest someone should see some embarrassing personal item.

"Pardon me," a familiar voice offered, bending down before her to help pick up the purse's contents. She saw a head of dark, shining hair before they stood and he handed her glasses back to her. "Here you go."

"Thanks." With sudden realization, she gave a self-conscious laugh. It was Trey, dressed to the nines in his most flattering dark, navy-blue suit. She'd seen him in it a thousand times, but the sight always took her breath away. The fit was perfection over his broad shoulders and tapered wonderfully to his slim hips without looking like it was trying too hard.

When he looked at her, his gray eyes took on an unusual light. "Have we met?" His voice was smooth and confident, but the thing that struck her was that it held no recognition whatsoever.

Was he joking? "Almost every day for five years."

His smile froze. His questioning eyes searched hers. "Jane? My God, is that you?"

She nodded and tried not to yank the scooped neckline of her dress up higher.

"Are you sure?"

She frowned. "What?"

He shook his head. "Nothing. It's just—nothing at all."

"Am I late?"

"No, not at all." He looked back at her. "I was early." Slowly, his eyes wandered over her, from her hair to her mouth down her body and back to her eyes. "You really look different."

She blinked. "I thought this dress would be okay."

"It is, it's…more than okay. I mean, you look terrific." He shook his head with a long, slow intake of breath. "Just great." He expelled the breath. "Wow."

She couldn't breathe at all. "Thanks."

He raked his hand across his hair and looked down for a moment. Then he looked back at her with an intensity in his eyes that took her breath away. "So, are you ready to go on with the show?"

"Yes."

"Then you'll need this." He dug into his pocket and took out a small velvet box. He opened it and took out a huge diamond ring. "As of now, you're my fiancée, so you'd better put it on." He handed the ring to her.

She took it. It was the largest diamond Jane had ever seen. It even felt heavy in the palm of her hand. "I'm a little nervous about taking responsibility for this."

"Go on. It's just for dinner. What could happen?"

She tried the ring on her trembling hand. "It's a

little loose," she said, noticing how easily it slid over her knuckle.

"We could have it—" Trey stopped himself. "I mean, if anyone were to notice it didn't fit we could say we were going to have it sized."

Jane nodded and took a steadying breath. "This must have cost a fortune."

"Somewhere around thirty-five thousand bucks." He looked at the ring. "It seems like a lot for a chunk of carbon."

"How on earth can you afford such a thing?"

He gave a rueful smile. "I can't. It's on loan from a jeweler friend of mine." He hesitated and they both considered the weight of his words. "I'm returning it in a few days."

"I'll be really careful." She let out a pent-up breath. "Okay, what should I do? Come in with you now, or join you in a minute after you've settled down? That way, it wouldn't look like we've been standing here plotting."

He snapped his fingers. "Good point. Yes. I'll go in now and you come in after me and make some excuse about the weather or something delaying you."

"Right."

He caught her by the wrist and looked deep into her eyes. "Are you sure you want to go through with this?"

She nodded solemnly. "I do."

The words hung before her in the air for several minutes after he'd gone.

Chapter Three

She waited for a tortuous five minutes before going through the dining room to the table where Trey and his father sat.

Trey stood as soon as she approached the table. "Sweetheart," he said, drawing her hand up to his chest to turn her toward him.

Her pulse pounded madly, right to her fingertips. She was sure he could feel it.

He put his other hand on her hip and gave a half-smile. "Sorry, but we have to make this look good," he whispered into her ear.

Before she could ask what he meant, he pulled her against him and lowered his mouth onto hers, muffling her startled exclamation.

"Make it look real," he murmured against her mouth. His aftershave mingled with their warm breath. Jane breathed it in like life-giving oxygen, and surrendered to the thrill of his kiss. Blood pounded and coursed through her veins with the rocket power of adrenaline.

Trey trailed his hand down to the small of her back, drawing her closer to him for just a moment. In reality, the kiss lasted no more than a few seconds, but to Jane it was a tingling eternity.

He pulled back and gave her a devastating smile, his hand still resting casually on the small of her back. "I'm so glad you made it," he said, in a normal conversational tone.

"Me too," she gasped, eyes wide. She blinked. "You have lipstick—"

"Where?" He swiped at the wrong place.

"No, just—there." He stood while she reached out and smudged the dusty-rose off his lips. When her thumb touched the corner of his mouth she had to force herself not to linger. Instead, she pulled her hand back, too quickly. He seemed to notice.

"Gone?" he asked, a little bemused.

"Yes."

He smiled easily and turned with her. His hand burned a patch of heat into the small of her back then trailed off as he stepped aside as if to showcase her.

"Dad, this is my fiancée…Jane Miller." His voice actually rang with pride. He was a better actor than she thought. "Jane, my father."

The elder Breckenridge stood and gave a half bow. He had a thick mop of gray hair and the same strong jaw and straight nose as his son. His eyes were blue and clear. "Lovely to meet you, my dear. I've waited a long time for this.'' He continued to stand as Trey pulled the chair out for Jane.

I know what you mean, she thought. She was surprised to hear her own voice sounding calm. ''I have too. Trey has told me so much about you.'' She paused and realized that her pounding heart seemed to have pounded some confidence into her. ''How are you enjoying life in the south of France?''

His expression broke into pure pleasure. ''Delightful. Wish I'd made the move years ago. I have a small, stone farmhouse, several dogs, goats, and all the peace and quiet I could ever want.''

''It sounds heavenly.''

''It is. I've been trying to get Trey to come and visit but he's always so busy.''

She nodded and tried to deflect the criticism from Trey. ''Do you play *boule?*'' She'd seen them playing the French version of Italian bocce ball on television and thought it looked like fun.

Terrence Breckenridge's eyes widened. ''As a matter of fact, I'm second in the village. There's one old-timer there who just cannot be beaten, though the Lord knows I've tried.'' He gave a laugh. ''Do you play?''

She shook her head. ''But I'd like to give it a try someday.''

''I know just the place, and just the man to take you there.'' He winked at Trey then said to Jane, ''Enough about me, I want to know all about you. My son has been very secretive.'' He gave Trey a pointed look.

Jane took a quick breath. ''What would you like

to know?'' This was where the improvisation was going to begin. She said a silent prayer that she would manage without bungling everything for Trey.

"How did the two of you meet?''

She felt Trey's eyes on her and spoke carefully. "At work. We've known each other for several years but we only recently…recently discovered—''

"That we're in love,'' Trey finished, laying his hand on top of hers. He must have noticed it trembling because he asked, under his breath, ''You okay?''

Jane could barely breathe. "Fine,'' she whispered back.

"Just realized it, eh?'' Terrence asked Jane with raised brows. His expression was unreadable, but in exactly the way that Trey's expression often was.

She swallowed and gathered her nerve. ''Sometimes when you work with someone for a long time you don't realize where business ends and personal feelings begin.'' She looked at Trey, sending signals with her eyes and with her heart that she knew he wasn't picking up on.

"Yes,'' Trey said, as if he'd given it some thought, which she was sure he hadn't. ''Sometimes you need the proverbial bolt of lightning to wake you up.''

Jane looked at him incredulously.

"Indeed that's true. I've seen it more than once in my lifetime,'' the older man said, taking the wine list from the waiter. He perused it for only a moment, then ordered. When the waiter left, he turned his attention back to Jane and Trey. "I had no idea the two of you had worked together."

"Yes." Trey cleared his throat. "Jane is actually my administrative assistant." He nodded, in a sort of marionette-like fashion, but didn't add anything to it.

Jane thought she'd never seen him so nervous. "You know how your son is, always burning the midnight oil to get things done. We've spent a lot of time working together in close quarters." She drew a tremulous breath. "I guess it was just inevitable that this would happen."

"Bah!" Terrence picked up a roll and slathered it with butter. "You could work together for years and never feel a spark, no matter how close the quarters. It's only inevitable when it's right. And I can tell just from looking at the two of you that it's right."

Jane smiled, uncomfortably aware of Trey next to her. "It seems to be," she hedged. *You could work together for years and never feel a spark.* His words stung with the truth.

The wine steward appeared and showed the bottle to Terrence for his approval. He gave a quick nod, then took the bottle from the waiter without bothering to take the customary sip of approval. "We need to drink a toast," he said, cavalierly sloshing the wine into everyone's glasses. "This is a sturdy little red wine from my new hometown, which I hope to introduce you both to very soon." He handed the glasses to Trey and Jane. *"Salut."*

They all drank.

"So," Terrence said, setting his glass down. "No

sense in beating around the bush. You two are thinking of getting married, eh?''

"Definitely," Trey said, too loudly, too quickly. He slipped his arm around Jane's shoulders and gave a squeeze. "I'm not letting this one get away."

Inhaling the clean scent of his aftershave, she nearly closed her eyes in ecstasy. Then she allowed herself the momentary luxury of sinking against him. With her arm pressed against his rib cage, she could feel the steady beat of Trey's heart. His body heat against her skin made her shiver with pleasure.

"I hope the lady agrees," Terrence said, with a questioning lift of his brow.

"Yes." With some effort, she straightened and took a bracing sip of the wine. "Ever since I met Trey, I've had the feeling he was the one," she said, more honestly than Trey would ever know.

The older man beamed delightedly. "So when's the date?"

There was a brief, awkward silence, then Jane said the only thing that came to mind. "February fourteenth. Valentine's Day," she added unnecessarily.

"Of next year," Trey put in quickly. Then, with a shrug to his father, added, "Jane prefers a long engagement."

Terrence looked at her. "Really, why is that?"

She felt the heat creep into her cheeks. "Why?" Her mind raced frantically. "Because..." She looked at Trey, whose face was curiously blank. "Because statistics show that people who are engaged a year or more typically have more successful marriages."

She thought she had read that, or something like that, somewhere. Sometime.

Beside her, Trey added an enthusiastic, "Yes."

Terrence scratched his chin. "I didn't know that."

"Oh yes." Trey picked up the reins. "Lots of studies have been done on the subject. The longer the engagement, the better the marriage."

The waiter appeared then to take their orders, and Jane took the opportunity to breathe and collect herself. She wasn't feeling as shy as she normally did in social situations. That was good. But she didn't feel certain about her acting skills. That was bad.

When it was Trey's turn, he hesitated over whether to get the chicken or the filet and Jane leaned in to whisper to him that the chicken dish was heavy on an herb he didn't like. "Remember? At *Chez Guisline* you said the tarragon tasted like soap leaves to you."

After a long, questioning moment of looking at her, he ordered the beef.

"That's what I like to see," Terrence said, apparently oblivious to Trey's silent query. "A woman looking out for her man. Call me old-fashioned, but it does my heart good."

"Jane is old-fashioned too," Trey interjected. "I just knew you two would hit it off."

They both looked at him.

"In what ways am I old-fashioned?" she asked.

"Loyalty," Trey said, letting his gaze linger on her for an extra moment.

"That's an important quality in a wife," Terrence agreed.

"That's an important quality in anyone," Jane said, just as Trey began to say the same thing. They exchanged glances.

"You took the words right out of my mouth," he said, eyeing her steadily.

Suddenly there was an exclamation of surprise and Jane, who was lifting her water glass to her lips, was knocked soundly by an older woman passing by. The water spilled across her lap and onto the floor.

"Oh! I'm so terribly sorry!" the woman exclaimed.

Jane took her napkin and started blotting the water up. "It's okay. It's just water."

"I just feel terrible," the woman said, reaching down with a handkerchief she had taken from her purse and blotting at Jane's skirt. "Just terrible." She bumped her hand soundly against Jane's, and the heavy diamond cut into her skin.

Her companion, a distinguished-looking man with dark gray-flecked hair and pale skin, wearing a slim-lined suit looked over the woman's shoulder at Jane and said, "This is my fault, really, I was rushing my wife out the door."

The woman continued to try and clean Jane up, embarrassing her further. "Honestly, it's okay. I can take care of this," Jane said, her hand knocking against the woman's again and knocking her black patent leather purse to the floor. "Oh, I'm sorry."

"Quite all right, dearest." The woman stepped back and reached awkwardly for her purse. When she regained her composure she was a little red-faced from the exertion. She opened the purse. "Please, allow me to pay for dry cleaning."

Was there no end to this embarrassment? "No, honestly, it's okay."

"If you're sure…"

Jane put a hand to the woman's and pressed the purse closed. "I'm sure."

"Oh, my, I feel I should do something," she blustered.

Jane looked to the woman's companion. "It's fine, really."

He smiled and took the older woman's arm. "Come along then, Rita, I have to get outside before the meter runs out." To Jane, he added, "Again, I'm terribly sorry."

She smiled. "Don't worry about it."

He smiled back and ushered the woman out of the restaurant.

"Quite a little wake-up, eh?" Trey said. "Are you sure it's okay?"

"Most of it got on the floor," Jane said. "My skirt is practically dry already."

"Good. All of this has reminded me that my own car is on a meter out front." Trey looked down and dug in his pockets for coins. "I'd better go and put some more money in or my car will be towed."

"I did it on the way in," Jane said, laying her napkin over the still-soaking stain on her lap. She turned her attention back to Trey and smiled. "You always forget the meter."

"Really." He looked at her with genuine interest. "I never realized that."

She nodded. "So when I saw your car out front on my way in, I checked and, sure enough, you only had a couple of minutes left."

He looked at her directly. "Your efficiency has always impressed me."

They were interrupted by the waiter arriving with their food.

"Efficiency," Terrence piped up with a chuckle. "Is that what strikes you most about your lovely fiancée?"

"Sometimes," Trey said lowly, eyes still on her. "But she's full of surprises tonight."

His gaze persisted, sending tingles of pleasure up and down Jane's spine, until she looked down.

"So." Trey turned back to his father. "I wanted to talk to you about the future of the company," he began, leaning forward to get down to business.

His father held up a hand. "We can talk about that later. Right now I want to know more about the future for you and this charming lady who has agreed to marry you. I hope you've discussed children." He nudged his son with his elbow.

Trey gave a brief, practiced smile. "We haven't discussed it yet."

Jane noticed Terrence's face take on a look which, on his son, meant skepticism so she said, "Beyond agreeing that we both want at least one, that is." What was she doing? Perpetuating this lie was bad enough, but to bring children into it—even imaginary children—was worse.

Yet the old man's expression softened to one of such pleasure that she found herself continuing.

"I'd like two, I think, but you know Trey. For him, more is better and he'd like three or four." She gave a little laugh. "We may argue about it until it's too late."

Terrence laughed with her. "You know, it's funny you should mention that because he's always been that way. I remember when he went to camp as a young boy—"

Trey looked stricken. "Oh, no. No, no, Dad, no childhood stories. Please."

"There's another thing," Jane said, enjoying the act. It was the first time in five years that her mental cache of personal facts about Trey would really come in handy. "He's so modest. He almost never talks about himself or his childhood traveling all around Europe."

The older man sobered. "I'm afraid that's my fault. Thanks to my work he was shuffled around quite a bit when he was a boy." He took a bite of his roll and waved it at Jane, adding, his mouth full, "As I'm sure you know."

"Dad, I haven't told Jane—"

"I know he started boarding school at Carlisle when he was in first grade," Jane said smoothly. She looked at Trey with a small smile. "Wasn't that what you said?"

His mouth was open in evident shock. "Yes." He turned to his father. "I told her that. You see, she already knows all about the old days. No reason to re-hash them now."

His father ignored him and leaned across the table toward Jane. "Did he ever tell you about the time in college, when he made the game-winning touch-down?''

Trey opened his mouth to object, but Jane beat him to it. ''Yes, in the last three seconds, no less. Stanford had a lot to thank him for his entire senior year, from what I understand.''

''Indeed,'' Terrence said proudly. ''That's my boy.''

Trey looked at Jane, shocked. ''I don't remember telling you that,'' he said, almost under his breath.

''You did,'' she reassured him in a low tone. In fact, he hadn't. She'd read much of it in the person-nel newsletter when they did an article on him sev-eral years back. His father had provided the details.

As the dinner drew on, Jane was able to work a lot of personal knowledge about Trey into the con-versation. This, at least, was one subject she felt con-fident about. She knew almost everything there was to know about Trey Breckenridge. Working with him day in and day out had given her almost a wife's knowledge of the man.

Her nervousness subsided as they talked, and she found Terrence to be surprisingly easy to talk to. He wasn't at all the dour founder of Breckenridge Con-struction that company lore had made him out to be. Stories held that he was a ruthless businessman, an exaggeration of the type A personality, but Jane found him relaxed and amusing.

Unfortunately, though, Trey was neither of these tonight. His tension seemed to rise in direct propor-tion to his father's ease. Jane longed to lay a reas-suring hand on his arm, the way a real fiancée would, but she didn't. She couldn't forget that her real place was as his secretary, not his fiancée. Such intimacy would have been inappropriate.

At the end of the meal, Terrence wiped his mouth with his napkin and dropped it onto the table. Then he beamed at them both and said, "I must say, I was a little dubious about this engagement at first, son."

"You were—"

He held up a hand before Trey could finish. "I know, I know, it was an unfair suspicion to have. Call me a paranoid old fool, but I actually worried that you might be rushing into a marriage in order to placate me into signing my shares over to you."

"Dad." Trey's handsome face was pale and serious. "I don't know what to say."

"No need to say anything. It wasn't a reflection on you, I think, but on me." He shifted his watery blue gaze to Jane. "You see, Jane, in the old days I might have done anything, no matter how drastic, just to keep the business running under my control. I had a control problem at the time. Very bad. Cost me a lot, and I don't mean money."

Jane saw, clearly, that he had once been a mirror image of his son. She could also see that it seemed to please him tremendously to believe his son was not like he used to be.

"Whatever our differences," he said to Trey. "Your mother raised you to be a fine man."

Trey shifted uncomfortably. "Dad—"

The older man held up a hand. "No, no. Let me say this now. You're hardworking and honest, two things I admire greatly in a man. But you've also taken the time to enjoy life and the people in your life.'' He looked at Jane and his expression softened into a smile. ''I admire that most of all.''

Her stomach twisted. He wasn't describing Trey any more than he was describing himself.

''I may not have been the greatest parent in the world,'' he went on. ''In fact, I'm sure I wasn't. But it has always been my chief worry that you would become trapped in the same work grind that kept me from you all those years. Now I see that my worry was wasted.'' He gave a rueful laugh. ''I suppose it was just my ego, expecting you to make the same mistakes I did. Nothing is more important than family. I know that now. Nothing. I'm sorry to have let you down.''

Trey's face had lost some color. ''That's all ancient history.''

''That doesn't mean it doesn't matter.'' He ran a hand through his gray hair in a gesture that reminded Jane of Trey. ''If I could go back and do it again differently, I would. Believe me, son, I would.''

Trey shifted in his seat. ''I don't harbor any resentments.''

Terrence shrugged. ''I hope not. I know you thought it was unfair for me to withhold the stock until you'd settled down, but maybe now you understand.''

''I think I do,'' Trey said, without inflection.

A lump rose in Jane's throat and she felt as if she had shrunk several inches in her seat.

The older man nodded. ''Now that I see what a lovely lady you've picked for yourself, I believe you do." He gave Jane a smile. "I hope you realize how lucky you are, Trey."

"Yes, of course."

Terrence returned his gaze to his son. "Then what else can I say? I think now that you're finally going to have a secure family life, it's time you took the reins of the company. Tomorrow I'll have our lawyer draw up the papers, and what's mine of this company will be yours."

Trey smiled, and it took Jane's breath away. "You won't be sorry," he said, extending his hand to shake his father's.

Again, the man looked at Jane, and she felt herself shrink even further. "I'm certain I won't." He patted his stomach and yawned. "Now, if you'll forgive an old man his frailty, in my village it's the small hours of the morning and I need to get to bed."

Trey stood. "We'll drive you back to your hotel."

"Nonsense. I'll take a cab. You two stay here, enjoy your time together." He gave Trey a penetrating look. "I'm not so old I can't get back on my own."

If Trey recognized the message beyond his father's words, he didn't show it. "No, of course not." Trey put his hand on Jane's shoulder and sat down. Her skin tingled where his warm fingers had touched her.

With one final, approving smile, Terrence walked over and took Jane's hand. "Goodnight, my dear. I can't tell you how very glad I am to have met you."

Jane struggled to find her voice. "It was my pleasure, sir. Goodnight."

They watched him walk out of the dining room

with a vigor that was unusual for a man his age, particularly one with jet lag. "There must be something in the water over there in France," Trey commented idly. "I've never seen him so energetic." He leaned back and sighed. "Well, I'm glad that's over with."

Jane looked at him miserably. "Do you feel as horrible about it as I do?"

"Horrible?" Trey looked incredulous. "Are you kidding? I feel great. The evening was a complete success. We had him utterly fooled, and now he's going to sign over those shares without any more nonsense."

Jane's heart sank. She knew there was a tenderness in Trey, she'd seen glimpses of it enough over the years, but she wasn't seeing any of it now. "I know, but he's doing it because he thinks we're so happily involved that he doesn't have to worry about you anymore."

"And he docsn't." He signaled the waiter for the check.

"Oh?"

Trey looked at her evenly. It was clear he thought she'd crossed a line, but amazingly she didn't feel she had to back off.

"Doesn't he?" she persisted.

"No," Trey said coolly. "I'm a grown man, I don't need my father," he looked at her pointedly, "*or* a wife—imaginary or otherwise—to look after me."

"Okay." She shook her head. "You're right, you don't."

A few minutes passed in silence.

Trey broke it first. "That was brilliant, by the way, what you said about the tarragon. How the hell did you remember that?"

"I like tarragon," she answered numbly. "I thought it was weird that you didn't."

He laughed and poured more wine in both their glasses. "And the Stanford football thing—where did that come from?"

"The company newsletter."

He nodded and raised his glass to her. "Jane, you are a genius. I don't know how I can ever thank you enough for this. You deserve a raise."

"No, I don't."

He frowned. Refusing money was a sure sign of something being amiss in Trey's eyes. "Jane, come on, we're on top of the world. What's really the matter?"

"I just deceived a really nice man in a big way, and I don't feel very good about it," she confessed heatedly.

Trey looked taken aback. "I don't think I've ever seen you angry before."

She gave a half shrug. "I'm angry at myself." She took her napkin from her lap and laid it on the table by her plate. "I think I'd better go."

"No, wait." He put his hand on her arm again, and this time it wasn't for show but because it was a natural impulse.

Jane waited, with bated breath.

"This was a good thing." He looked at her with as much sincerity as she'd ever seen in his eyes.

"You know I'm not really getting married but you said yourself that believing I am made him stop worrying about me. So what's wrong with giving an old man some peace of mind in his golden years?"

"Do you really believe that or are you just trying to make me feel better about what we've done?"

He didn't hesitate. "I believe it completely. More importantly, I have the company and a hundred employees to worry about. Things haven't been good these past few years and we owe a lot of money, but with Davenport lined up, and dad unable to veto the deal, we're going to be fine." He paused. "Just fine."

She looked at him for a long moment. "I hope you're right."

"Believe me, I'm right." The waiter came back with the bill and he handed over a credit card. "Can I give you a lift home? First I've just got to make a quick call to my machine..." He reached for his inside pocket.

"No, thanks, I have my car." She opened the clutch and took out her keys.

"Okay, then." He paused and looked deeply into her eyes. "Thanks again, for everything. You really saved my life tonight."

Her cheeks flushed. "I don't think that's true."

He took her hand in his. "It's true," he said. "And I won't forget it."

She could only stare back at him.

The waiter reappeared, then, with Trey's card and credit slip. Trey took it and fumbled for a pen. "I guess I'll see you tomorrow,'' he said to Jane, reaching for his pocket again.

"Right," she said flatly. "See you bright and early."

It was over. The clock tower was striking the midnight hour and it was time for Cinderella to go back home in her pumpkin. Or, in this case, her Ford.

"Wait, Jane."

She stopped and turned back to him. "Yes?"

He gave an embarrassed smile. "I seem to have forgotten my cell phone, do you have yours?"

"Oh. Sure." Of course she did. She was always on duty.

She opened her small purse and took out the small phone and handed it to him, their fingertips brushing as she did.

He didn't seem to notice. "Thanks." He dialed a series of numbers in and listened. He saved a couple of messages, but when he got to the last one, his face grew very still. As he listened, he slowly went pale.

"Trey, what is it?" Jane asked, as he clicked the phone shut and muttered an oath.

"My father left me a message on his way back. He had a great time tonight."

She didn't get it. "Good."

"So great, in fact, that he's going to stay a little longer than expected. He wants to spend more time with us."

Now she got it. Their one-night charade was being extended indefinitely. She sat back down next to him and, very seriously, said the first thing that came to her mind—a characteristically practical question which sounded insignificant the moment it was out of her mouth. "What about the ring? Don't you have to give it back?"

He looked at her for one puzzled moment, then laughed. "That, Jane, is the least of my worries."

Her face grew warm. "Yes, I suppose you could ask your friend for an extension of some sort."

"Right. At the moment I'm much more concerned about what it will take to convince my secretary, who is a tremendously professional woman as well as a splendid actress, by the way," he laid a hand on her shoulder, "to be my fiancée for just a little bit longer."

Tiny shivers ran up Jane's bare arms, though whether it was from his touch or from his proposition, she couldn't say. "You could try just asking her."

Smile lines crinkled at the corners of his eyes. "She'd have to be crazy to agree."

"Maybe she is crazy and you just don't know it." Jane shrugged. "There could be a lot of things you don't know about her."

He studied her for a moment and his smile slowly faded. "Would you, Jane? I'll try to keep the act to a minimum but can I count on you to be at the ready to perform, so to speak, in the meantime?"

She smiled reassuringly, ignoring the voice inside her that said she was betraying herself and that she'd never be able to keep up this act without huge emotional risk. "Yes, Trey. You can count on me."

Chapter Four

When Jane got home half an hour later, Peatie was waiting for her on the living room couch, draped in a large, cotton throw and watching an old movie on the TV.

She pointed the remote at the set and Cary Grant blipped into oblivion. "What happened?" She patted the cushion next to her. "Come on, I want every detail."

Jane dropped her purse on the hall table and walked into the living room. "Well." She sank dreamily onto the sofa next to Peatie. "It was wonderful." She paused, remembering Trey's intimate touches and the thrill of pretending, just for those few hours, that they had a real relationship. Her skin flushed with pleasure despite herself. "It was really wonderful."

"You're going to have to get more detailed than that."

Jane smiled, remembering. "When I got there, he gave me this gorgeous diamond ring—"

"A ring!" Peatie grabbed her hand to examine it more closely. "Fabulous!"

"It's only a loaner." There was no surprise in that information, yet when she heard herself say it out loud, Jane felt her heart grow heavier. "Temporary. Just like the whole arrangement."

"We-ell, it seems to me the fact that he gave you the ring at all is pretty symbolic of something."

"He loaned it to me, after a jeweler friend of his loaned it to him. For the night. It's symbolic of the fact that he needed me to look like his fiancée, that's all." She looked off into space, remembering her first sight of the ring glittering in its box. "But it was fun anyway."

Peatie laughed. "So he gave you the ring and…?"

Jane told Peatie the whole thing, from the delightful repartee with Trey's father, to the fact that Terrence had agreed to sign his shares over to Trey in the morning, right through to the look on Trey's face when he realized they were going to have to keep up the charade for a few more weeks.

"I think horror is probably an exaggeration," Peatie said.

"He was definitely not pleased."

"So it's a game," Peatie concluded, waving off Jane's dismay. "Like the ultimate game of dress-up. Enjoy it."

"I can't, because this is drudgery for him," Jane said, sinking deeper into the soft cushions of the couch. Her tight muscles relaxed fractionally. "I can't enjoy it knowing that we're not playing the same game. I'm playing out a fantasy, yes, but he's playing for his life and he's miserable.''

''So you're going to have to show him that, with you, this game is fun. Show him life with you is fun.''

Jane gave a wry laugh. ''Right. How?''

''With your winning personality, the warmth of your affection, your terrific shepherd's pie and your certainty that you are right for him.''

''You really think I can win him with sheer determination?''

''You can if fate is on your side, and, Jane...'' Peatie paused dramatically. ''I think this time fate is definitely on your side.''

Despite everything, it was good that Jane had been there tonight, Trey decided. Really good.

He was at home, standing on the terrace of his penthouse condo in an old building called The Gables. It was one of Breckenridge Construction's greatest renovations and usually it gave him great pleasure to look over the city from this vantage point.

Not tonight, though. For some reason, tonight he was feeling as if he were standing on the edge of a cliff after drinking a bottle of vodka. Sure, the evening had been a success as far as winning his father's approval for the night went. But how could he keep the act up? How could he and Jane keep convincing his father that they were in love when, in some important ways, they barely even knew each other?

He pictured Jane in his mind and wished she was

with him right now. She'd soothe all his misgivings. She had such a knack for stabilizing his chaotic world. Tonight she had been smooth and confident, and she'd carried the evening right through to its successful conclusion. That was her talent.

He leaned against the railing and looked across the landscape of city lights, twinkling like gems. What would Jane say to him right now?

She'd probably come up with some plan, that's what she'd do. She'd figure out all the pertinent information they'd need about each other as an "engaged couple," and she'd type up a cheat sheet for Trey in case he found himself in a position where he had to demonstrate his knowledge. Then she'd fill his schedule so full of appointments—everything from his annual physical to having his teeth cleaned—that there would be virtually no time for him to go out with his father and his "fiancée" again before the old man had to go back home to France.

He should call her, he thought, turning to go inside. The sooner she got started on this, the better.

He stopped. It was late. He looked at his watch. It was really late. She'd be asleep for sure. He couldn't wake her up just because he was feeling a little insecure.

He could wait until morning. She'd be there for him then. If there was one thing he could count on, it was Jane and the fact that she was always—always—there for him.

If anyone could help pull him out of this mess of deception he'd created, it was her. There wasn't a lot he had faith in, but he had faith in Jane. She'd never let him down. For years she'd juggled bank accounts in bad times, and kept public relations going smooth in good times. No matter what the need, Jane seemed to know how to fill it. Business-wise, they complemented each other perfectly. He was big picture, she was detail. He knocked over the boulders, but she cleaned up the resulting gravel and made things sparkle.

He rolled his eyes. Jane would have come up with a better analogy than that.

She was indispensable.

He really had to give her a raise.

"Your father's waiting in your office," Jane told Trey in a hushed voice as he walked into the office the next morning. Gone was the musical, laughing voice of last night. She was in her cool efficient mode again.

"He's here now?"

"Yes, surely you remembered he was coming by to sign the shares over." She let out a delicate breath, her shoulders relaxing beneath a creamy, silk blouse.

She glanced down and Trey found himself momentarily fascinated by her long, dark eyelashes and the curve of her high cheekbones. How could he have gone all these years without noticing how attractive she was?

"When you were...Trey?" She raised a hand self-consciously to her face. "Why are you looking at me that way?"

"Sorry, I was just...thinking. Go on."

"Listen, with you coming in so late—"

"Late? I'm not late, he's early." He looked at his watch. "It's not even nine o'clock yet."

"It's nine forty-five."

"What?" He looked at the digital clock on her desk then back at his own watch. Noticing the second hand wasn't moving, he muttered an oath. "What next?" he asked, raising his eyes heavenward.

"That's just what I was getting at. When you were late and I didn't know why, your father came to the conclusion that we'd had a little lovers' spat." She glanced at the door to Trey's office and lowered her voice to a whisper. "I couldn't convince him otherwise."

Trey thought quickly. "There's a guy selling roses on the street corner. Occupy my dad for just a few more minutes while I run down and get some, then I'll bring them in as a conciliatory gesture. It might help explain why I'm so late for our appointment."

"Can't you just tell him your watch is broken?"

Trey scoffed. "Not good enough."

"Wait, I don't want him thinking we're this bickering couple."

Trey stopped and looked at her, puzzled. "What does it matter?"

She clasped her hands in front of her. "It just does."

Trey had no patience for this. "Then we'll tell him it was a dignified fight." He dashed toward the door. "I'll be right back."

When he got back to the office, his father was sitting easily on the sofa in his office and Jane was perched nervously on the edge of Trey's desk.

"...really, I wish you wouldn't worry so much about us," Jane was saying. "I'm sure Trey will—well, here he is now."

Trey produced a stunning bouquet of yellow roses and baby's breath. "Jane, these are for you. I'm sorry."

She gasped and then glanced nervously at his father. "Th-thank you."

"Dad," Trey said, turning to the older man. "I apologize for being late, but I'm afraid Jane was a little irked at me, you know, a woman thing, and I felt it was important that I apologize first thing this morning." He felt Jane straighten up behind him.

"I wasn't irked with you, Trey," she said crisply. "I told you that."

He turned and saw a tiny hard glint in her eye that he could read perfectly: she didn't want the blame being laid on her. It was really kind of cute. "You're right," he said, and turned back to his father. "I was actually a bit irked with her."

"What?" she asked, incredulously.

He gave her his best smile. "But that's all over with now, so, Jane, perhaps you'd like to put those in water."

"What on earth could this delightful young lady have done to make you angry?" Terrence asked broadly, ready to defend Jane no matter what. "I can't believe it."

"Yes, what did I do that made you angry, Trey?" she said. He noticed the beginnings of a smile nudging at her lips. She looked very pretty.

Funny he'd never noticed that before.

"You know..." Trey frowned, scrutinizing her. Was her hair different? Was she wearing a new outfit? He gave himself a mental shake. He had serious concerns right now, why on earth was he trying to figure out if Jane had a new wardrobe or hairstyle? It must be the stress.

"No, actually, I don't," Jane said.

He was on the spot. "You know, the whole business of the, ah, the, ah, the football season." He turned to his father. "Jane's afraid the Cowboys are going to take too much time away from the two of us being together." He gave an aren't-women-silly shrug.

"And he doesn't want to come to the games with me," Jane interjected, with a guileless shrug of her own. "That's right. I thought it would be such a perfect way for us to spend time together that I got season tickets, but he'd rather stay home."

Trey sent a shocked glance her way. She'd trumped him. Slowly he turned back to his father. "So, you see, it was really nothing."

"Well, it sounds to me like the girl's got a point there. Son, I thought you enjoyed going to the games."

"I do," he said to Jane.

She met his gaze evenly. "Then the problem is solved." Had her eyes always been that vivid shade? Had they always looked so sultry? Maybe it was just her glasses, magnifying them.

Had they always done that?

"Yes," he said. "The problem is solved."

"Thank you for your help on this, Terrence," Jane

continued. "Now I really should put these flowers in water and let the two of you get down to business."

Trey watched her go with a grudging admiration, then dragged his thoughts back to the matter of the stock transfer. "Did you bring the papers?"

"Of course, of course." Terrence sat up and took some papers out of his briefcase. "Now, you'll see that part of this is a non-taxable gift transfer, under tax code…"

Trey found his gaze drifting back toward the door where Jane had just left. She was really something. So quick and witty. She wasn't about to let him make a fool of her.

"…part will be taxed at a rate of forty-two percent, which was the best we could…"

He tried to focus on his father's words, but couldn't. What in the world was the matter with him? Suddenly he felt as nervous as a schoolboy around Jane. Jane, for Pete's sake! He'd seen her every day for years with barely a personal thought. *Stock,* he said to himself. *Controlling interest. The Davenport job. Concentrate!*

But it was one final thought that brought his attention back—saving Breckenridge Construction and all the jobs of the people who worked there, Jane included.

Twenty minutes later, after an exhaustive explanation of every paper he had, Terrence seemed no closer to signing. At least not by Trey's broken watch.

"You know," Terrence said, pen poised over the documents. "Spending even this short amount of time at the office this morning reminds me of why I left it all in the first place.'' His voice was calm, measured, and without doubt. ''I wonder how benevolent it truly is for me to sign it all over to you.''

Trey's face froze in uncertainty. ''Things aren't usually too chaotic.''

''Chaotic enough, as I recall.''

''My best work comes when I'm under pressure.''

Terrence snorted. ''That's a lie, the same one generated by thousands of people who are afraid to let go of a little control in their lives.'' He must have seen the weary surprise in Trey's eyes because he went on to say, ''But I can't tell you what to do any longer. If you really want this, I'm not going to stop you.''

Relief poured out in a rush of breath. ''Thanks.'' He glanced at his father's unmoving hand. ''Did you want another pen?''

''No, I've just remembered we need a witness.''

Automatically, Trey slapped his hand down on his desk buzzer. ''Jane, could you come in here please?''

A moment later she was in the door. ''What can I do for you?'' She shifted her gaze to Trey and held it for a moment. He noticed she made just the slightest hint of a smile, and he gave a small nod of acknowledgment.

''We need you to witness our signatures,'' Trey explained.

''Should I bring some coffee in?'' she asked. Her eyes held the same sort of gleam as the diamond on her left hand.

Trey smiled, and, for the first time that morning,

really meant it. "You don't need to bother with that sort of thing, Jane. You know that."

Her gaze eased from Trey to his father. "How about you, Terrence? Juice? Anything?"

"No, thanks. I try to limit my morning intake of food and fluids. Find it keeps me even-tempered." He glanced at Trey, with a bossiness that was becoming increasingly annoying. "You should try it."

"I'll do that." Trey clenched his jaw and counted to three. This was the beginning of a new life for him, a stronger position in the company. Things would only get better from here. He just had to make it through the next fifteen minutes.

"All right then." Finally, with great flourish, Terrence signed the documents, passing them, one by one, to Trey to sign. At the end, Jane signed the dotted line as a witness and the deed was finally done.

"Now, I'd like to explain these papers to you one more time," Terrence said ponderously.

"If you'll excuse me," Jane said. "My phone has been ringing off the hook out there. I think I'd better go see what's so urgent."

"Thanks for coming in, Jane," Trey said, smiling.

She smiled back, and it was beguiling. "Of course."

Behind her in the outside office the phone began to ring again. "There it goes. I'll let you two wrap up the last of your business."

She disappeared, and Trey turned his attention back to his father, though he was dying to get down to the business of adding up the shares and finding out what his total holdings were.

Unfortunately, first he had to endure the lecture one more time. "If you look here," Terrence began slowly, "you'll see that part of this is a non-taxable gift transfer, under tax code..."

Given the way everything else had gone over the past twenty-four hours, Trey shouldn't have been surprised about the total of his father's shares combined with his, but he was shocked.

"Forty-eight percent," he said slowly, staring at the paperwork before him. "Forty. Eight. Percent." When he raised his eyes to his father, the older man shrugged.

"When you turned eighteen I gave you thirty percent of the shares," his father said, in a tone of recrimination that Trey remembered well. "With this thirty, you should have been fine. What happened?"

The sound of the phone ringing in the outer office was the only thing that broke the silence. Trey watched the blinking line flare to solid red as Jane answered the phone.

"What happened to your thirty percent?" Terrence asked again.

Trey groaned inwardly. If he'd known his father only held thirty percent himself, he never would have cashed in any of his shares, even when he was eighteen, and young, and foolish. "I sold some a long time ago."

"For what?"

He hesitated, watching the buttons on the telephone light up and blink as Jane, in her office, obviously juggled the lines. "Call it a bad investment."

"I should say so. What did you need so badly that you had to sell your stock?"

This was relentless. Trey leaned back in his chair and felt the black cloud that had been over him for twenty-four hours surround him like a bad smell. "It was an automotive investment."

His father's expression shot from confused to comprehending in an instant. "It was that old Ford, wasn't it?" The older man shook his head. "I knew you weren't working enough hours at the pizza place to pay for something like that."

"It was my money." It was impossible to be defensive about such a stupid move. "And the shares were much cheaper then. At the time I thought it would be easy to earn a little more money and buy the stock back."

"It doesn't work that way with this kind of company. Unless you have someone who's willing to sell, you can't buy."

Trey clenched his jaw. "I realized that shortly afterwards." He shook his head. "But that's not doing me any good now."

"Did you ever get that car roadworthy?"

Trey pinched the bridge of his nose where a headache was rapidly forming. The car had been beautiful, on the outside. A classic. It had run exactly one hundred and eighty-four miles before dying on the highway. After that it hadn't made it to a hundred miles without having one major problem or another.

"It's a moot point now, though," his father conceded.

"I couldn't agree with you more."

"So approach some of the other shareholders to buy," his father was saying. "See if you can make up the difference."

Trey returned his attention to the man across the desk from him. Finally, a subject he was comfortable with. "The shareholders I can identify refuse to budge, and the rest are practically untraceable." An idea surged in him. "Although if there's anyone who could trace them…" He hit the intercom buzzer on his desk. "Jane."

"Yes?"

"Come in here for a moment, would you?" He glanced at his father, noticed the sharp-eyed expression, and added a feeble, "Sweetheart."

There was a momentary pause, then, "Something has come up. I'll…I'll be a couple of minutes."

Trey scowled. What could have come up this time? What could possibly be going wrong now? "Well, just as soon as you can, then. Oh, and Jane," he tried to clear the uneasy lump from his throat, "Sweetheart, do you happen to know where a list of the company shareholders is?"

Another split second pause. "I—I think there's one in my files."

"Bring it with you, please."

"All right but…" The line crackled with silence. "I'll be there in a moment."

The minute he lifted his hand off the buzzer, his father said, "That's interesting."

It was exactly the sort of comment, the sort of tone, Trey would have loved to ignore, but had never been able to. "What's interesting?"

"You treat her more like an employee than a fiancée."

A tiny bubble of patience burst in Trey's brain. He let out a weary breath, then looked at his father soberly and said, "We've always kept our personal lives out of business and it would make everyone uncomfortable if we suddenly stopped now." Real uncomfortable.

Terrence stood and walked across the floor to an oil portrait of himself. He studied it for a moment in silence, then turned back to Trey, apparently unaware of the disturbing specter of himself looming over his shoulder like a cartoon of the devil. "What happens when she's your wife?"

"What do you mean?"

"Will you still keep your personal lives separate?"

Trey watched his father's expression. "That would be awkward."

"Indeed."

"I don't think we need to worry about what's going to happen after we're married. Jane and I are very clear about our relationship."

Fortunately she walked in before Terrence could press for further details. Trey held his arm out to her, and she handed him a folder.

"Thanks." He opened it and pulled a sheet out.

"There's something I need to tell you," Jane started.

"Just a minute." He held up a hand and scanned down the sheet that contained a list of names and percentages held. "Twenty-two percent, six percent, ten percent, five percent, eight percent, three percent." He scoffed, then froze and looked closer. Three percent. When he'd looked this over before, some of the smaller percentages seemed irrelevant, but now that wasn't the case. "Three percent is owned by JAM, Inc." He looked to his father. "Do we know what JAM, Inc. is?"

"Never heard of it."

"Jane?" He looked at her. "See if you can look that company up."

She didn't move. "What do you want to know?"

"I want to know exactly who they are, where they are, and, most importantly, if we can slip their three percent out from under them."

Her cheeks flamed red.

"Jane?"

She swallowed visibly then dropped a bombshell. "JAM, Incorporated is me."

Chapter Five

"*You?*"

She nodded. "My initials. JAM."

Terrence appeared thrilled. "Then together your wife and you will own controlling interest in the company." He sighed with deep appreciation. "Clearly this proves the validity of my plan."

Trey tried to keep from glowering. "Yes," he said through his teeth. "It seems it does."

Jane cleared her throat delicately and said, "I'm afraid there's a problem. A rather big one, and it just can't wait."

Dread lodged in Trey's chest. "What's wrong?"

She shot a doubtful glance at Trey's father. "It's about Rankin Securities."

"Go ahead."

She pulled a chair up beside the desk. "Dick Monroe just called. Rankin is calling in the loan he gave you."

Trey was dumbfounded. "He can't do that."

"What's this about a loan?" Terrence asked.

Trey hesitated, then said, "A year ago I had to get a substantial loan to keep the company afloat. A substantial personal loan."

"A personal loan? Why didn't you get a corporate loan?"

"Because no one thought the company was a good risk."

The older man shook his head. "Son, no company is worth the risk of personal bankruptcy."

"This company is," Trey returned vehemently. "All we needed was to get a big job, like the Davenport hotel bid we just won, and it would clear the loan."

Terrence frowned. "Davenport?" His frowned deepened. "I'm not aware of a deal with Davenport."

This wasn't going to be easy. "I didn't discuss Davenport with you because you would have nixed it and, Dad, we needed it desperately."

His father must have heard the truth of this because he didn't argue. "All right, then why isn't the loan cleared?"

"Because they haven't paid yet." He turned his attention to Jane. "We wrote Rankin and asked for a deferral, didn't we?"

She nodded. "Unfortunately the answer is no."

"Wait a minute," Terrence interrupted, with a deep frown. "Did you say Rankin securities? Philip Rankin?"

Jane looked at her note pad. "Yes. Philip Rankin."

Trey dropped the folder onto his desk. "Do you know him?"

The older man's face grew red. "I know him all right. I have for years. Why the hell did you go to him?"

"I had no choice. We needed the money."

"But why him of all people?"

"Why not?" Indignation rose in Trey. "I know you were never a great fan of his, but he's a longtime shareholder with a stake in the company. He seemed like the ideal candidate."

Terrence was now steaming. "Think about it. He's a shareholder. He gives you a huge loan, knowing that your assets—including your shares in the company—are your collateral. You miss one payment and bingo! He owns controlling shares."

Trey felt his face go cold. "There's something you're not telling me, isn't there? For some reason this business between you and Rankin is personal, right? Why would he want control?"

"It is personal." His father's voice was harsh. "He used to date your mother."

For one suspended moment, Trey couldn't comprehend what his father had just said. "You're kidding."

"Indeed I'm not."

"Good God," Trey groaned. "If there's one thing I should have learned to expect by now, it's the unexpected, but this," he shook his head and gave a short laugh, "this is a surprise." He raked his fingers through his hair. "When?"

"Now, son, we were separated at the time. It was when you were about ten years old. She came back to me and broke it off with Rankin. Not long after that, she passed away and his chance with her was gone. He's been out for revenge ever since."

"You have got to be kidding." It felt like a helium balloon was expanding inside Trey's skull. "I'm being forced into bankruptcy because of a twenty-seven-year feud over Mom?" He laughed again, but this time, to his own ears, it verged on hysteria.

A door in the outside office opened, and Jane stood up.

"Who's that?" Trey asked.

"That should be Dick Monroe," she said. Her voice was as calm and soothing as hot tea. "I called and asked him to come over." She opened the door and poked her head out. "Come on in, Dick."

Jane came back in the room. "Dick has already spoken with Mr. Rankin and he'll be able to tell you a lot more than I can," she said, ushering in a short, plump man with artificially dark, bushy hair. Fortunately, what he lacked in judgement about personal aesthetics, he made up for in legal savvy. Which was why Trey paid the man a huge retainer to be his personal lawyer.

"I was about to call Jane myself when she called me," Dick said, setting his briefcase on Trey's desk and reaching across to shake hands. "How are you doing, Trey?"

"I don't know. How am I doing?"

"Not too great." Dick turned to Terrence and extended his hand. "Terrence, good to see you." He turned back to Trey with a grave expression. "I don't often use this expression, gentlemen, but someone is really out to get you."

"Yeah." Trey gestured for Dick to sit in the vacant chair opposite him. "The question is, can he do it?"

"He certainly can." He snapped open his briefcase and took out a sheaf of papers. "This is a copy of your loan agreement. Your cure time of fifteen days is up tomorrow. The money is owed, in full, first thing on Wednesday morning."

Trey looked at his watch. "So as of now, no legal action has been taken against me. I'm still current."

"Technically, yes. Until midnight tomorrow, when you lose three million dollars' worth of personal assets."

Trey glanced at Terrence. "Isn't there some saying about the sins of the father coming back to haunt the son?"

"If there wasn't already, there is now," Terrence said, with obvious contrition. He turned to the lawyer. "Dick, is Trey's job in danger?"

Dick gave a quick shake of the head. "Not as long as the company's intact."

"I suppose that's something," Trey said heavily. He didn't really believe it, though.

"Don't count on it," Terrence said cynically. "He tried to shut us down years ago. When he didn't succeed at that, he bought in, hoping to gain control that way. He doesn't want to own a construction company, he wants to own me and he's doing it through you.''

Trey opened the folder Jane had brought in earlier. ''Rankin owns twenty-two percent right now. With my shares he'll own control.''

''But with Jane's shares, you'll own control,'' Terrence reminded him.

Trey scoffed. ''Not by midnight.''

Dick watched this exchange, then said to Trey, ''Declaring bankruptcy is still an option. Actually,'' he appeared to shake off another idea, ''it's probably your only option.''

Probably. ''Is there another?''

Without cracking a smile, Dick said, ''You could get married immediately and transfer your assets to your wife before this goes into action tomorrow.''

Trey was about to reiterate the fact that he was sunk when Terrence's eyes lit up. ''Well, you and Jane will just have to push the wedding date up, that's all there is to it.''

Dick frowned. ''Trey and Jane?''

Terrence gestured broadly and Jane shrank back. ''Jane Miller. She and Trey were planning on marrying next year, but under the circumstances they should probably push the date up.''

''Way up,'' Dick said, still frowning as he looked from Jane to Trey and back again. ''I'm sorry, I had no idea the two of you were engaged.''

''Not many people know about it,'' Jane said shortly.

A light of comprehension came into Dick's eyes.

"I think I understand. So how would you two feel about getting married immediately?"

Trey felt a trembling in his chest. "What do you mean immediately?"

"I mean hopping on a plane and flying to Las Vegas or some other city that doesn't require a waiting time between licensing and marriage and doing it tonight."

He tried to swallow. "Tonight?"

Dick nodded. "Unless you can do it sooner. As I said, this would all have to take place—power of attorney, transfers, et cetera—by tomorrow."

"That shouldn't be a problem, should it, son?"

The room seemed to spin. He glanced at Jane, who looked as pale and shocked as he felt. "Why so—so dramatic?" He tried to laugh. "I mean, really, tonight? Doesn't the law allow for some sort of grace period?"

Dick folded his hands before him and leaned in toward Trey. "Not with signed loan papers like these. The wheels that could roll you right out of the driver's seat are already in motion. To mix metaphors."

"And I have no other recourse?"

"Apart from bankruptcy, no."

Trey took a deep breath and looked at everyone in the room. Suddenly it felt really crowded. He shot Jane a look and for a moment their eyes locked and he thought she understood.

She turned to Terrence and made some light comment about marrying in haste. Trey went to the water cooler in the opposite corner and tried to collect himself as he heard the quiet sound of nervous banter coming from the direction of Terrence and Jane.

Dick seemed aware of this, too, and followed Trey. "It's important," he said lowly, as if willing Trey to comprehend every syllable he uttered, "that the two of you know what you're getting into. If you have any doubts about staying married for as long as this takes, don't do it."

"How long will this take?" Trey asked, under his breath.

Dick shrugged. "Ideally it would be just a couple of weeks to clear the loan and start divorce proceedings. That's ideally. If for some reason you can't satisfy the loan that fast, you'd have to be married for as long as it took. If you were to get divorced before all your debts were cleared, this transfer could be deemed fraudulent and therefore unenforceable."

Trey blinked. "Meaning...?"

"Meaning you go to jail." He glanced back at Jane, who seemed oblivious. "Both of you." He lowered his voice and Trey knew in that moment that Dick had figured out the truth about them. "Now if this big job you got recently really pans out, you could be out of the hole before you know it. They couldn't touch you then. But even so, an uncontested divorce takes a year to become final."

"I hear you," Trey said gravely. Then he paused for just a moment and added, "Thanks." He walked back to his desk and said, in a normal conversational tone, "I think I need to talk to Jane alone."

"Of course." Dick picked up his briefcase. "As

long as you do understand that this matter is of the utmost urgency…?"

"I understand."

"Call me at my office before 4:30 this afternoon so I can draw up the appropriate papers."

Trey nodded soberly. "I'll do that." He watched his lawyer leave, then dragged his gaze back to his father.

"I have a feeling this is all going to work out just fine," Terrence said. He was suddenly looking surprisingly relaxed, under the circumstances. "For my part," he gave a creaky stretch, "I'm remembering why I wanted to leave the business in the first place." He stopped and took Jane's hands in his. "I said it before and I'll say it again—my son is a lucky man to have you."

She blushed prettily and looked down. "Thanks."

Terrence gave Trey a wink as he passed through the door. "Should I charter a jet?" he asked.

"I'll take care of all that."

"Naturally, I'll expect an invitation to the wedding."

"Naturally."

When the older man had left the office, Trey turned back to Jane with an unexpected nervousness. They were alone. Really, really alone. He shut the door with a resolute thunk behind him. Jane looked at him, with the expression of a guilty co-conspirator.

He splayed his arms. "I have no right to ask."

Her chest rose with a deep breath, then fell.

"You heard Dick—I need to marry someone and sign my life over to them. There's no one on this earth I trust more than I trust you.'' His brow suddenly pricked with cold perspiration. It was absolutely true. He'd never realized it before. He shook his head and walked over to the window. ''But this is serious business, with serious implications. We can't just quit if we don't like it. I can't think what you'd get out of the deal that could possibly make it worthwhile for you.''

''We-ell,'' she said slowly. ''I do have an investment to protect.''

''Three percent.''

''Hey.'' Her voice sharpened. ''That three percent may not seem like much to you but it's my nest egg...my future.''

He turned to her. She was flushed. Her chest rose and fell with quick breaths and her lips were parted, as though she was either waiting to be kissed, or about to speak again. ''What are you saying?''

She looked down for a moment, then raised her eyes back to his. Now she was definitely blushing. ''I'm saying if there's only one way to save the company, and I can help, I'll do it.''

''You'd marry me?'' he asked, getting right to the point. ''You'd give up your social life in order to pretend to be married to me?''

I'd give up anything to be married to you, she vowed silently. He was talking about what, under normal circumstances, would be the dream of her lifetime. It was as if he was asking her to take a bullet for him.

Of course, it wasn't the dream, it was only a mirror reflection of it, without any soul or meaning beyond the outward appearance. A make-believe marriage. Maybe that was worse than no marriage at all...but maybe it wasn't.

If she went through with it, at least, for one brief moment in her life, she'd have her dream. Sort of.

She searched for the right thing to say. "I'll do it if," she began, then stopped. The words weren't coming out right. But then, what were the right words for a situation like this? There probably weren't any. The best she could do was tell him yes before he decided it was too much to ask. She took a breath and tried again. "If you want to marry me, I'll do it."

Chapter Six

"Are you *sure?*" He looked surprised.

She tried to smile. "Sure. I think I can clear my calendar for you."

"But it could tie you up for a long time. I mean, the marriage would be quick but Dick said it would take a year for the divorce alone. I want you to understand fully what you would be getting yourself into."

"I understand perfectly. I mean, a year's not so long when you consider all that needs to be done for the company."

He raked his hand through his hair. "Maybe." His mouth tightened into a skeptical line, then he asked, "Are you sure you know what you're saying? Because if you're really willing to go through with this, it's going to save my life. I'm not going to spend a lot of time trying to talk you out of it."

She laughed. "Then say no more."

Trey went to his desk. "This is great. Just great. I'll call Dick and—by the way, he knew. About us, I mean, and how we're not really involved."

She nodded sagely. "I gathered. You could almost see the light go on." She hesitated, then added, "It didn't look like a casual water cooler chat you two were having. He was telling you this marriage business is a serious step, wasn't he?"

Trey nodded. "But it's good that he knows. He can draw up a contract for this marriage deal too without us having to explain our reasons."

"What kind of contract?"

"You know, a sort of prenup, laying out the guidelines we set. Something that sets up a settlement for you after the marriage. I really want to make this worth your while. I'll get Dick on it right away." He reached down to hit the buzzer that summoned her desk but stopped short, his hand hovering over the button. "Now this raises an interesting question."

Jane smiled and gestured at his hand. "About my job?"

He nodded. "I can't really have my wife acting as my assistant...can I?" He sat down heavily, picked up a pen, and jotted *assistant?* on the scratch pad by the phone.

She sat down too. "I don't know, but I can't afford to lose my job, even if it does save my shares in the company. I need that salary. I've got to pay for rent, food, tons of things."

"Jane, I plan to pay you for playing my wife, of course." He tapped his pen against his chin. "You do realize you're not going to be able to keep your apartment.''

She frowned. "What do you mean? The lease is in my name. My roommate needs my portion of the rent.''

"How's it going to look if we're married and we live in separate places?"

Her mouth dropped open. "You want me to *live* with you?"

He shrugged then grimaced. "This is getting awfully complicated."

Jane took a long breath, then reached across the desk for his pen and scratch pad. "Let's take it one thing at a time." She wrote *living arrangements* under where Trey had written *assistant?* "What other questions do we have to answer?"

Trey looked at the clock on the wall. It was three-fifteen. "How we're going to get this together on time for Dick to draw up the papers."

Jane glanced behind her at the clock, then back at Trey. "One thing at a time, Trey. You're always getting ahead of yourself."

She was right. "Okay, okay. What have we got? Your employment here, right?" He let out a long breath. "I'd hate to lose you as my assistant, Jane, especially at a time like this."

"Plenty of families work together, especially when it's a family business. Two of my doctors have their spouses working for them in an administrative capacity."

"Really? And the wives don't mind?"

Her mouth curled into a charming smile. "Well, only one of them is a wife."

Nailed, a voice in his head laughed. *Male chauvinist.*

"But no," Jane continued. "Neither of them seems to mind at all." She shrugged. "To tell you the truth, I don't want to leave my job either."

His eyes lingered on her smile. "What if you had kids?"

"That hardly seems likely."

"No, I just meant theoretically." His eyes locked on hers and a strange vibration ran through him. He quietly turned his attention to the *Ocean in a Box* on his desk. What in the world was he asking her that for? Maybe because he found himself wondering what Jane would look like, pregnant with his child. So the real question was, why was he wondering that? He was wondering because it was becoming rapidly apparent to him that Jane was a desirable woman. "I guess I was getting off the topic. What else do we have?"

"Living arrangements," she said, in a soft voice that cracked.

"Right. Living arrangements." He tipped the box and watched the water in it slosh back and forth for a moment. "Living arrangements," he said, returning his gaze to her face. "That one seems obvious. It's a big change for us both, but I don't see how we can tell the world we're married and expect them to believe it if we don't live together. My place is big. You'll have your own room and plenty of privacy." He pictured a white line down the center of the apartment, dividing it into his and her halves. "We'll figure it out."

Jane hesitated. "I'll have to continue paying rent at my apartment with Peatie. At least until she can find a new roommate." She smiled suddenly and snapped her fingers. "I'll put a sign up on the bulletin board in the lunch room. Not only will that reinforce the idea of our marriage to the folks around here, but hopefully I'll get someone I know and trust into the apartment."

She really did have a pretty smile. Had he been such a boorish boss that she hadn't smiled much around here before, or had he just never noticed? It seemed impossible to believe he hadn't noticed. He would have to have been blind. But then, maybe he was. "What about involvement with other men?" he heard himself ask.

"There's no one else," Jane said.

"Good." When her head jerked up, he added, "So we don't have that complication."

Two heartbeats passed then she asked, "How about you?"

"Me?" He scoffed. "Well, you know what happened with Victoria. No, there's no other woman in my life."

"Good," Jane said. "No complications there either."

"Nope. No complications." He tapped his pen on the desktop. "Are you agreeable to the term of a year?"

"That's not very—" She stopped, swallowed. "Whatever you think. It's fine with me."

Trey scribbled absently on the blotter pad before him. "There's the matter of what you take out of this."

"I don't need to take anything out of it that I don't take into it," Jane said firmly. "I mean it."

"But, Jane, it's a lot. Getting married to me, holding the trusts in your name...I'm asking a lot of you."

"The alternative seems to be that I lose my job and my investment," Jane said simply. Her voice was no-nonsense suddenly. "It's good business."

Good business. Of course it was. He could see that. It was better business for him than for her, but if she was satisfied with it then so was he. There was nothing more to say. So why did he feel there was something missing?

He leaned forward and picked up the phone. "I'm calling Dick, then. I'll have him draw up the papers. Why don't you see if you can book a flight to Las Vegas, first class, then go home and get whatever it is that you'll need."

Jane pressed her lips together and nodded. Her eyes looked very bright.

"You're sure you want to do this?" Trey asked, certain that she was having cold feet and that the answer would be no.

"Very sure," she said, in a curiously light voice. She stood up. "I'll book that flight."

With that she walked out the door, closing it softly behind her. Left alone, Trey found himself wondering why, when he should be thinking about all the things that could go wrong with this plan, he was thinking about the wedding night.

Jane's movements were purely mechanical from the moment she walked out of Trey's office. She, Jane Miller, was going to marry Trey. It was incomprehensible. Tonight she would be Mrs. Terrence Breckenridge III.

She sat down at her desk and opened the phone book to the airlines section. So far it was no different from any other task she'd performed at work for the past five years. She called three airlines to compare prices, then called the best one back and booked two first-class seats to Nevada, paying more than she'd ever paid for an entire vacation.

The clerk asked for the names, she gave Trey's name without any problem. But when it was time to give her own, she stumbled, realizing that it would change before midnight tonight. A wave of emotion overcame her and she could barely choke out the words.

After she hung up, she sat back in her chair and took several deep breaths. *Relax,* she commanded herself. *This is part of your job, it's not for real.* Of course it wasn't for real. None of this was for real—how could it be? Dreams didn't come true this neatly. At least Jane Miller's dreams didn't.

Nevertheless, there on the paper before her was the confirmation number for two seats on an outbound flight to Las Vegas. It was going to happen.

Her deep breathing technique did nothing to soothe her frantic heart, so she had to do the next best thing. With a trembling hand, she lifted the telephone receiver again and called Peatie.

"WestTex Cable."

"Peatie, you have to meet me at home right away."

"Wha—"

"You just have to, I'm desperate."

"Jane? Is that you?"

"It's me. I think it's me. Anyway, it's someone who looks like me, although her life is totally different from mine."

Peatie's voice sharpened. "What's wrong?"

"Nothing's wrong." She tried to breathe but it was like sucking air through a straw. "Really. My whole life is about to change, and I've got three hours to prepare for it, but other than that, I'm just fine."

There was a momentary pause. "You'll have to give me another clue, because I'm just not getting it."

"In three-and-a-half hours I'll be on a plane to Las Vegas." The voice was hers but she could hardly believe the situation was. "I'm getting married. Tonight."

She heard Peatie's gasp. "To who?"

"Trey."

Peatie gasped again. "No! You're kidding, right?"

"I'm not kidding and it's too complicated to get into now. Just meet me at home, help me get ready, and I'll tell you the whole story."

"Jane, wait, is this for real?"

"It's true, but it's not for real."

"Huh?"

"I'll explain when I see you. Bye." Jane hung up the phone and looked at Trey's office door. Was he in there now, regretting having asked her? Was he trying to figure out a way to tactfully tell her never mind? Something inside told her that he was. He had to be.

But was she going to sit around like a bump on a log waiting for him to come out and reject her? Maybe the old Jane would have but not the new Jane. Not the Jane who was about to be Jane Breckenridge. This Jane had to get home and do everything she could to live up to the name she was about to adopt.

It was time to say goodbye to Plain Jane Miller.

Peatie's work-place was five minutes away from their apartment, so by the time Jane had driven the thirty-plus minutes to get there, Peatie was already waiting for her.

"How long do we have for your makeover?" Peatie asked as soon as Jane walked through the door. She was holding a hairbrush in one hand and her box of makeup in the other.

"We don't have enough time for a makeover, I can tell you that." Jane dropped her purse onto the hall table and consulted her watch. "I only have two hours before I have to leave."

"Great. We can do this." Peatie set the makeup down, took Jane by the arm, and pulled her down the hall to the bathroom. "I've been wanting to do this for ages."

"What are you up to?" Jane asked, warily eyeing a box of hair highlighter that was on the counter.

Behind her in the mirror, Peatie feigned innocence, poking her thumb at her chest. "Moi?"

"Toi." She nodded at the box on the counter. "That's not the same stuff you use."

"Well of course not, silly, my hair is way too light to use that shade." Peatie smiled devilishly. "No, that's for you."

"For me."

Peatie nodded. "We're going to highlight that breathtaking beauty you think you don't have but which you actually do."

"And the magic is in that box."

"Some of it." Peatie nodded. "And don't worry, I know what I'm doing. Did I ever tell you I went to cosmetology school?"

"No."

"Well, I did and tonight you're going to reap the benefits of my education."

"I don't know..." Jane looked at the pretty, happy-looking model on the cover of the box. There was water behind her, and just the tiniest sliver of a yacht. Clearly anyone who used this product was destined for a world of sunny days at costly marinas. She sighed.

Trey had a boat.

"No, this is crazy, I'm not going to fall for this," she said aloud.

"Fall for what?"

"This," she gestured at the picture, "this suggestion that if I change the way I look, it's going to change my life and make everything right.''

''Well, your life has already changed. Now you need to change with it.''

Jane looked at Peatie in disbelief. ''I'm on my way to my wedding. What if this doesn't work? What if it turns my hair green or something?''

''I can assure you that won't happen. Look at this,'' she held the box out to her, ''it says right here that it's subtle.''

Jane gave a wry smile. ''More subtle than you?''

Peatie rolled her eyes good-naturedly. ''Infinitely. Come on, Jane, it'll be fun.''

Jane raised her brow. ''Did you like to play with dolls when you were little?''

Peatie frowned. ''Uh-huh, why?''

''I'll bet all your dolls had chopped hair and red pen around their mouths, am I right?''

Peatie's face colored. ''How did you know that?''

Jane laughed. ''I had a friend just like that when I was little. As soon as she brought a new doll home she had to get to work on it, just like you want to get to work on me.'' She considered the box again and sighed. ''All of my dolls had chopped hair and red lips too. You know why?''

''No, why?''

''Because I wasn't brave enough to do the cutting and coloring myself, but I wanted my dolls to be as glamorous as hers so I always handed them over to her.''

''Does this mean,'' Peatie's smile was broad, ''that you're handing yourself over to me?''

Jane hesitated, waiting for the last of her caution to blow away. When it didn't, she pushed it away and said, "Yes, I'm all yours. But you'd better hurry before I change my mind."

Peatie clicked her tongue against her teeth and shook her head. "You know, I am seeing a whole new you lately, Janie." She took the box from the counter and ripped the top off. "I don't know what it is, but in all the time I've known you I've never seen you take a chance of any sort."

"Things are definitely changing." Jane said determinedly. "From now on I'm going to be a risk-taker."

"Thatta girl." Peatie dumped a packet of powder that came with the highlighter into a plastic bowl, then opened a small bottle of what smelled like ammonia and poured it in, stirring with what looked like a narrow toothbrush.

Jane wrinkled her nose as the scent wafted to her. "You promise this isn't going to be too dramatic?"

"Nah." Peatie shook her head. "It's just to warm up your natural tone. You go put your robe on and come back."

Jane went to her room and closed the door behind her. Tonight she was going to become Mrs. Breckenridge, at least in name. Every time she had the thought, even knowing it was a sham, her body tingled with anticipation. Mrs. Terrence Breckenridge III.

How she wished it was for real! She wished that tonight was going to be her wedding night, and not just the night she and Trey went through the motions of marriage. But that was all it was. This was business. It was almost funny to think that a marriage of convenience could still exist in modern society.

She shrugged into her robe and took one last look in the mirror. She looked the same as always, and yet there was something unfamiliar about her reflection. Perhaps it was that she'd never looked that closely before.

"With any luck," she said to herself. "When Peatie's finished, I'll look like the real me. The me I've never been before." A smile filled her. "Maybe this is the beginning of a new life for me."

An hour later, Peatie had worked a miracle—at least it felt that way to Jane.

Now they were going through Jane's closet, trying to find something suitable for her to wear.

"I still can't believe it," Jane said, running a hand through her newly cut hair. It was still long, although Peatie had cut a good six inches off, and had layered it into a flattering frame for her face. "This feels so funny. I wonder how long it'll take to get used to."

"You'll stop thinking about it in about an hour," Peatie said with a smile.

Jane beamed. "I think you're right. Oh, Peatie, I wish you could come."

"I do too, believe me, but if I'm not at work in the morning, they'll have someone else at my desk by afternoon. By the way, who is going? The new father-in-law?"

Jane shook her head. "I called him but his back has gone out. The disappointment in his voice was

just heartbreaking, but he insisted that we have another ceremony, maybe to renew our vows on our
first anniversary.'' She clicked her tongue against her
teeth. ''I hate to think how disappointed he's going
to be when we dissolve the marriage after everything's straightened out.''

''Maybe you won't.''

''Don't start, Peatie. This is a business contract
only. When the term's up, the term's up.'' She hesitated, then added softly, ''Whether I like it or not.''

Peatie raised her eyebrows knowingly. ''We'll see.
So,'' she said, turning her attention back to Jane's
closet before Jane could argue, ''what are we going
to do about your wardrobe?''

Jane was glad for the change of subject. ''What's
wrong with my wardrobe?''

''Nothing. My grandmother would love it.''

''Very funny.''

''Look, you've got this great figure, you're young
and pretty, why not have some fun with your
clothes?''

''Fun like that sort of fun?'' Jane gestured toward
Peatie's T-shirt. It was a silk-screened torso of a
man's hairy chest.

''No, I don't think this is your style.''

''Good.''

''You're more of an Audrey Hepburn type, I—and
others—would say. How about...'' she scanned the
closet, ''this one?'' She took an off-white dress from
a hanger. Jane had bought the dress for an occasion
several years back, but she could no longer remem-

ber what the occasion was. Whatever it had been, it hadn't been worn because the tag was still on it.

After Peatie zipped the dress, Jane stepped in front of the mirror. The dress hugged her form in all the right places, and the shoulders and neckline dropped seductively low. Now she remembered why she had never worn it. "Don't you think this is a little...over the top?" she asked Peatie.

"It's gorgeous," Peatie said vehemently. "It's just stunning on you."

Jane cocked her head and tried to study her reflection objectively. The woman she saw barely looked familiar. Her hair was falling in soft waves around her face, her make-up was subtle but highlighted her large, pale eyes and the cheekbones that were so much like her mother's. The dress was very feminine and pretty. It fit well, without pulling or gaping anywhere.

All in all, she was pleased with what she saw. And that kind of pleasure was something she wasn't used to.

"What do you think?" Peatie asked behind her.

"I think..." Sudden tears filled Jane's eyes and made her throat constrict. She looked down for a moment and bit her lip, trying to stop the onslaught of emotion from spilling over the makeup Peatie had applied so carefully. "I think," she repeated after a moment, "I'm too hopeful. I may be setting myself up for a huge fall."

"Oh, no. No, you're not. This is going to be great."

"It's going to be business."

"It may start that way, but it's going to have a happy ending."

"Why do you think that?"

"I did your Tarot cards." She said it as though it was proof positive.

"Peatie, I have to be practical."

"Fine. Be practical. Just be open to things changing, okay? Go with the flow."

"All right." She pressed her lips together. "What if he sees all this hope in my eyes?"

Peatie leveled her gaze at Jane and said, quite seriously, "He'll find you enchanting, but he won't know exactly what it is."

"You really think so?" Jane asked softly.

After a moment, Peatie answered, "I really, truly do." She swiped her hand across her cheek and gave a sniff. "Now, come on, let's get a trousseau together and get you out of here. You have a wedding—"

Jane held up a hand. "You mean a marriage. Big difference."

"Okay, a marriage." Peatie smiled in a way that reaffirmed everything she'd just told Jane she believed but there was a touch of sadness in her eyes. "You have a marriage to go to tonight, but I have a feeling about you and Trey. That it's going to turn out to be real."

Jane drew in a breath. For a long moment she was silent, allowing herself to believe it. Then she exhaled and shook her head. "No, Peatie. I wish you were right, but you're not. Trey and I are boss and loyal assistant, nothing more. And even though we're getting married, that's never going to change."

Chapter Seven

The smell of leather was overwhelming in the rental car. Jane thought it must be a scented spray, because it was too pungent to have occurred in any natural way. Yet it went perfectly with the blur of neon as they drove down the main drag of Las Vegas Boulevard.

Unbelievable. It was 10:00 p.m., yet outside it was as light as day. Throngs of people crowded the street like Manhattan at lunch time. She'd never been anyplace as universally incongruous. The strangest part of it was that, possibly for the first time in her life, she felt certain that she was exactly where she was supposed to be.

As weird as everything was on the outside, she felt safely cocooned inside the car with Trey and everything felt right. It was as if they were traveling around this frenetic city in a haze of magic and romance. Which was ridiculous, she knew, but that's the way it felt.

She looked out the window and marveled at the different people walking along the sidewalk. It was like Halloween. Women wore sequined dresses, with poofed-up hair. As they drove, Jane counted at least five women with the same false red hair color, and wondered if next they would pass a beauty parlor boasting a specialty in 'auburn' coloring.

Trey slowed the car to a stop at a red light and drummed his fingers on the dashboard.

She touched her fingers to her hair and remembered how long she and Peatie had worked on it. So much for the big makeover, she thought wryly. Trey hadn't appeared to notice any change in her at all. In fact, he was barely looking at her.

Jane focused on a man crossing the street. He was wearing a powder blue leisure suit, the legs of which were just a little too short. His face was unremarkable except for the slightly discordant bush of black hair on top of his head.

"Nervous?" Trey asked Jane, in a quick, tight voice.

"A little bit," she answered. "You?"

"Nah." The drumming of his fingers grew faster. "Piece of cake. Keep your eyes open for a chapel."

"We've already passed three."

"Really? I hadn't noticed."

"You don't want to do this."

"Yes. Yes, I do. I have to do this." She had just a few moments in which to feel hurt, before he reached over, touched her forearm, and said, "I didn't mean that the way it sounded. Honestly, I am so grateful to you for agreeing to this."

She tried to be casual, to show that she was no more attached to the romance of this than he was. "All in a day's work."

He laughed. "If I'd known you were that committed I would have taken advantage of you long ago."

It was a perfect opportunity to flirt but she hadn't the vaguest idea what to say. "What do you mean?" she asked, and immediately set about a mental flogging of herself. Of all the things she could have said, the flirtatious or suggestive quips she could have come up with, that was the least provocative.

"I mean, this is what happens when you stay faithful to one company for too long. You sometimes have to marry the boss."

Her spirits rose foolishly. "Funny, I don't remember that in the contract."

"Fine print. Very fine print. Nearly invisible."

Remain cool, she told herself. *Act like it doesn't matter so much.* "Seems to me I typed the contract myself."

"That's exactly what I wanted you to believe." The light changed, and he accelerated abruptly.

"I feel like I'm trapped in some weird dream," Trey mused. "The Twilight Zone."

"I've been thinking the same thing. If you pinch me, I'll pinch you."

He raised an eyebrow at her. "Is that a warning, Miss Miller?"

They both chuckled thinly then fell into nervous silence again. So much for small talk.

Jane sighed and turned to watch the scenery pass from the side window. It was all so surreal. And yet, in some inexplicable way, it all made sense. It fit together smoothly in that weird manner that dreams often did. Artificial smell, artificial lights, artificial hairpieces galore, and an artificial marriage.

It wasn't the way she'd envisioned her life when she was a little girl, but then neither was pining for her boss for five years in a secretarial job. Life was an impossible thing to predict and plan. The sooner she accepted that, the better off she'd be. This may not be a dream come true, but it was undeniably a change. And perhaps a step in the right direction…especially if Peatie and her silly Tarot cards were correct.

"I guess we can stop anytime," Trey said, surveying the landscape before him. "Just say when."

"Me?" She balked. He may as well have told her to give the orders for a firing squad.

He must have heard the hesitation in her voice because instead of questioning her, he explained, "I've got to keep my eyes on the road."

Jane sighed and sank back in the seat. It was going to be a long night. It already had been. Part of her wanted to put off the marriage so she'd have at least a little more time to get used to the idea, but the fact was that they didn't have the kind of time she'd need to get used to it. How could she get used to marrying—even as a sham—the man she was in love with?

With that in mind, she decided they'd probably both be better off if they did it quickly.

"There's a place," she said, pointing to a jutting neon sign that said Drive-thru Marriages $25.

Trey glanced over and groaned. "You've got to be kidding."

"Why?"

He gave a wry laugh. "It's so...look at it."

She tried to see what in particular he was objecting to, but it looked just like the twenty-five other chapels they'd passed. Surely Trey wasn't being sentimental about this. "What's the difference? One chapel is the same as another here, right?"

He made a face. "Even under these circumstances, I'd rather not get McMarried."

Hope flared but she was quick to squelch it. *Don't read encouragement into every little thing he says.* "So it's not as elegant as a chapel full o' Elvis, is that it?"

"I don't know. Even that's a little better than just driving through."

Jane studied him. "I don't think you want to go through with this," she said again, this time more certain.

He shot her a sidelong glance. "Are you saying that because you don't want to go through with it?"

"No, I'm saying it because I don't think you want to."

"Well, I do." His voice grew louder.

Her nerves must have been more raw than she thought because Jane found herself raising her voice as well. "I do, too."

"Good."

"Good." This was one of the stupidest arguments she'd ever had.

"I just don't think you're the kind of woman that a guy marries at a drive-thru, even if it is more convenient."

She was slightly taken aback. "What sort of woman am I then?"

He shrugged self-consciously. "I don't know. You strike me as more of the white wedding on dad's arm with the whole town watching sort of girl."

She swallowed. "And what about you?"

"Me? I'm not the marrying type."

Her delicate bubble of hope burst. "That's exactly what I've been saying."

He pulled the car over abruptly and turned to face her. "Look, I'm the first to admit I'm not the marrying kind. What's more, I'm the first to admit that you deserve a hell of a lot better than this, but the sooner we both remember that this is business—that white dresses and daddy's arm don't have anything to do with this—the better off we'll both be."

She looked at him hotly. "I do realize it, Trey, that's why I pointed out all those places where we could stop and get it over with."

He let out an exasperated sigh. "There's got to be something a little nicer than that, even here."

She smiled. "The sooner you remember that this is business…"

He looked over at her and smiled. "You must think I'm crazy."

She shook her head. "No, I think you're a little too gallant for these surroundings yourself."

"So what do we do?"

"We realize where we are and what's it's like and we just deal with it."

"Good plan." He started the ignition again. "Do you see anything out there? Anything at all. I won't hold out for the National Cathedral."

She laughed, then looked at the building they'd stopped in front of and gasped.

"What?"

She pointed. "Right there. Look."

They were in front of a looming, white Victorian-style house. There were lacy, red hearts strung along the balcony, with gold paper rings intertwined. The sign—possibly the only one in Las Vegas that wasn't neon—was hard to read in the dark but it said—Love Byrd's Sweetheart Chapel. Then, in smaller letters, it said Open 24 hours. Rev. Pamela Byrd presiding. Except for the fact that it was right next to a strip-mall, it might have been a quaint Justice of the Peace.

"What do you think?" Trey asked.

Jane's first thought was that fate had finally inter-vened on her behalf. "It's fine."

Trey took a deep breath and gripped the steering wheel hard. "You ready?"

"I guess so."

He released his grip and switched off the ignition. "Let's do it, then."

Inside, the chapel was so filled with heavily scented flowers that it made Trey feel lightheaded.

A tinny-sounding piano played the wedding march, just a little off-key, like a piano in a ragtime movie. Solemn-faced couples waited on polished wooden pews, holding hands and whispering who-knows-what to each other.

Unfortunately, it was still Las Vegas, and a dewy-eyed couple, both with pierced faces, stood at the front while a woman with hair like cotton candy stood at the altar asking them if they promised their souls to each other forever.

Trey felt his forehead break out in a cold sweat. This felt wrong. There had to be another way.

Yet Dick had assured him that there wasn't.

A lump lodged in his throat and no amount of dry swallowing seemed to help. It was just nerves, he told himself. Perfectly normal, under the circumstances. He was getting married, albeit in name only. It was still unfathomable. And so sudden—who wouldn't be disconcerted? Twenty-four hours earlier he'd been on top of the world, with no idea of the desperate measures he would have to take today.

He glanced at Jane, next to him, and immediately rescinded his last thought. She was too good to be considered a ''desperate measure.'' Granted, as they'd already discussed in the car, she wasn't a genuine glowing bride, but she did deserve some special regard for going through with this.

Though she did seem to glow.

Why was that? Trey's chest constricted. Until this moment, he'd felt they were comrades, the only two in this town who were out of place. Now, seeing her look, for all the world, like a bride, he felt like he was the one who was out of place. Again, he had the thought that she deserved so much better than this.

She was staring straight ahead at the couple getting married, and her eyes had softened apparently in direct proportion to his own heart hardening. Looking at her, watching the gentle rise and fall of her chest, and the way her hands were folded neatly in her lap, eased that somewhat.

Jane always made him feel more at ease. If he had to get married—as he obviously did—she was the most comforting person he could have at his side. But then, she wasn't merely at his side, she was getting married too, to him. Yes, it was finite. No, it wouldn't really change their lives that much, but still it was a big deal. Why didn't she seem more uncomfortable with the idea?

What was going on with her all of a sudden?

All his anxiety returned and coiled in the pit of his stomach. After this was over, how could they ever go back to their normal employer-employee relationship? It would be like thanking the person who just saved your life and then telling them to fetch you a cup of coffee. They couldn't go back to that, could they?

If not, he would lose the best assistant he'd ever had. It was an unfortunate consequence but there was nothing he could do about it. Together, they had controlling interest in the company. Apart, they would each own small shares of nothing. They had no choice.

"You've got to take a number, Sweetie." The distinctly New Jersey voice which brought him back to the moment came from a small, thin woman behind a white podium by the door. Her hair was molded into a beehive, and her face had the extra-alert look of one who'd consulted a bad plastic surgeon. "Yo," she snapped, because apparently he was staring. She whipped a number out of a deli-counter machine and handed it to him. "Wait over there. We'll call you when it's time."

He looked at the number she'd handed him. Sixty-six. "I don't like this chapel," he whispered to Jane.

"Why not? I'm sure it's better than all those other ones we passed."

He searched for some feeling he could put into words, glanced at the number in his hand, then from corner to corner of the suffocating room. "There's no Elvis."

She flashed him a sympathetic, yet bemused, look. "I'm sure you could grab one off the street outside if you really wanted to."

"It's not just that, it's…it's—"

"Fifty-nine!" The crepe-necked woman barked.

"It's that. And all this." He swept an arm across the scene before them.

Jane shrugged. "This is Las Vegas, after all. This is as close as we're going to get to finding a Norman Rockwell wedding chapel here."

"That's exactly it," he whispered back. "Despite the fact that this isn't a real wedding I want it to be better than this. More elegant or something. More traditional. Where's the kindly old minister? Where's the apple-cheeked woman in a pale blue dress, with pale blue hair, who's supposed to be playing the organ?''

"They're in Wisconsin somewhere," Jane said, then smiled. "And they'd never condone what we're doing."

He had to laugh. "You're right."

So theirs was not a traditional marriage—did that necessarily mean it should be so untraditional? He thought about that for a moment, then decided it did. This was perfectly appropriate, considering what they were doing.

"Trey," she whispered to him after a moment. "We forgot about a ring. I think they're selling them over there." She pointed to a glass display case behind the woman who had given them a number when they came in.

"It's all right, I've got one," he said.

She looked at him, surprised. "You do?"

He gave a half shrug. "I grabbed it on my way out this evening. It might not fit, but..." He dug into his pocket and produced a small gold and garnet ring. "Let's give it a try."

She extended her left hand to him and he took it in his own. Their fingers curled into a light grip for a moment and he looked into her eyes. "I can never thank you enough for this."

"Don't worry about it." Her voice was barely a whisper. "It's just a game, like playing dress-up or something."

"Here goes." He slipped the ring on. It was a little tight going over the knuckle but he forced it on. "It'll work."

"That's lucky." She examined it more closely. "Trey, this is beautiful. It's got to be an antique."

"It was my mother's."

She looked at him, shocked. "Your mother's? I can't wear your mother's wedding ring."

"It was the only thing I had." He was like a kid, defending himself. "What's the big deal? We needed a wedding ring and it's a wedding ring. Problem solved."

"It's too special." She tried to pull the ring off. "Oh, no."

It was the last thing he needed to hear. "What's the matter?"

"Trey, it's stuck."

"What?" He pulled. It didn't budge. He pulled harder. "It is stuck."

"I know." She drew her hand back. "I'll have to leave it on because if we yank any more my finger will swell up like a sausage."

"You think it's an omen?"

"What kind of omen? A good one or a bad one?"

He thought about it. He had been thinking it might be a sign from above that they were definitely supposed to go through with the marriage, but now he wondered. "I don't know. It could go either way."

"Sixty!"

A couple stood up and shuffled to the front, leaving an empty spot on the pew in front of Trey and Jane. As they hurried up the aisle, Trey heard the man say, "Shut up, I'm doing it, aren't I?"

Jane sat down silently and Trey joined her. The waiting area was cramped and Jane was pressed against him. "Sorry, there's no room," she whispered.

"I'm sorry to drag you into this whole mess."

She laid a hand on his forearm. "You haven't done anything to me."

"Except ransomed your livelihood and your nest egg. The more I think about it, the worse I feel for bringing you someplace like this."

"Trey, it's okay. Really." Her voice was like real music, in stark contrast to the caterwauling that was coming from the boom box. "People do this all the time, for all kinds of reasons. It's not that terrible. Besides, it will make a great story."

"You really mean that?"

She swallowed. That one hesitation said it all, but he couldn't afford to recognize it. He decided instead to believe her when she said, "Yes, I really mean that."

After that, they watched in silence while one unlikely couple after another made their way to the front and took the same vows.

For lack of anything better to do, Trey kept a mental tally of which ones he thought would work and which ones wouldn't. So far the score was five no's and one maybe. If they took odds on Vegas weddings, he could make a fortune.

But what right did he have to pass judgment? He was as bad as any of them, maybe worse, because he was intentionally going into a temporary union.

He wondered if his and Jane's insincerity was as obvious to everyone as theirs was to him. He glanced at Jane again. Her profile straight and dignified, despite their surroundings, the curve of her mouth classic and sensual. She was beautiful, she really was. She deserved the Norman Rockwell wedding, and the Norman Rockwell groom, instead of this....

He was stealing precious time from her. He was tying her up in a sham marriage for nearly a year of her life when she should be out, enjoying herself, enjoying being young and beautiful. How was it he'd never thought of her that way before? What a lousy time to develop a conscience about it. At least it wasn't too late.

"I can't do this to you," he said, taking her hand and starting to stand up. If he didn't do this now, he wouldn't do it at all. "Come on, let's get out of here."

Her grip tightened on his. "Stop it, Trey."

He sat down again and whispered, "I'm not going to use you like this."

"I told you not to worry about me." She pressed her lips together and glanced at the floor before saying, "I want to do this."

"You're a terrible liar. Your emotions are written all over your face."

Her skin turned pink when she looked back at him. "I'm not lying."

"Yes, you are. Now come on, let's get out of here before they call our number and I have to make a chivalrous announcement about how you've changed your mind and how devastated I am."

"No," she whispered harshly. "If we leave now and the lawsuit goes forward as planned, you stand to lose everything. Including my part of your everything,'' she added, before he could object. ''So let's just do this and get it over with.''

Gratitude filled him.

He hated feeling grateful.

''You're sure?'' he asked.

''I'm sure.''

''All right then, stop kicking up such a fuss.''

She turned an incredulous eye on him. ''Me?''

He smiled. ''Well, someone.''

''Someone,'' she said, returning his smile. ''I'll try and follow your model of decorum from now on.''

She was captivating, really. He'd never recognized her magnetism before. If he was the sort of guy to get married for real, she was just the kind of woman he'd want to marry.

''Good plan,'' he said, in a voice that wasn't quite his own. ''Just follow me.'' He tried to laugh. ''I know exactly what I'm doing.''

''Sixty-five!''

Jane started. Every time the woman bellowed a number, it surprised her. Fortunately, that part of the ordeal was almost over. She fingered the ring on her left hand nervously.

''Last call for sixty-five!''

For a moment, no one in the crowd moved, then someone called, ''Coming!'' from the back corner, where Jane hadn't noticed anyone before.

A man came forward pushing a wheelchair in which sat a delicate blond woman in a simple white wedding gown of the type being sold in the shop next door. On someone else it might have looked cheap, but on this woman it looked simple and elegant.

She watched as the unusually handsome man pushed his bride up the aisle, without a hint of self-consciousness—or doubt—on his face. The woman looked a little more tentative, glancing furtively at the people she undoubtedly knew to be watching her. She clutched a small bouquet of daisies that looked as if they might have been hand-picked on the way in. They were wrapped in a simple embroidered handkerchief.

As she wheeled past, her eyes locked with Jane's for an instant and Jane smiled. The woman smiled back, and the happiness transformed her face into a mirror of such joy that it struck Jane like a blow to the chest.

They stopped at the altar and the man walked to the side of the wheelchair and reached for his bride's hand. Both of them straightened and faced the minister with far more dignity than the surroundings warranted.

Jane watched as they took their vows, sounding as if they meant every single word they said. She'd doubted the success of the other unions she'd watched, but this one she felt no doubts about at all. Watching these two people, listening to the emotion in their voices as they spoke, gave her faith, while at the same time, making her feel that much more of a fraud. Yes, she'd mean every word she said to Trey, but what kind of fool was she to set herself up that way, knowing that he was just going through the motions?

She looked at him. He was watching the couple too. His jaw was set and she could see a small muscle ticking. Jane thought she saw a softness in his eyes that verged on tears, but when he looked at her his eyes were dry. "You ready?" he whispered, and she knew from his voice that he was moved by what he saw too.

She nodded, not trusting her own voice to be steady.

He covered her hand with his and nodded toward the couple at the altar. "Think it'll last?"

"Yes."

"Me too. It almost makes me feel funny to go up after them."

Jane swallowed hard. "Pretend you're in love."

"What, look miserable?" He smiled.

"Ha ha. Never mind."

"Are you scared?"

She took a short breath. Scared? That didn't even begin to cover it. "It will be over in a couple of minutes." She turned her attention back to the minister and didn't look back at Trey, even though she felt his eyes on her.

"Hey." He nudged her. "Did I say something wrong?"

"No, I'm just a little nervous."

The minister clapped her book closed and announced, "You may kiss the bride!" with exactly the same enthusiasm as she'd done with the six couples they'd already witnessed.

The man bent down with a smile that he could barely contain and they kissed tenderly.

Jane's eyes burned with unshed tears.

"Sixty-six!"

Trey squeezed her hand. "Here goes." He stood up and waited for her to do the same.

As they passed the couple who had just taken their vows, the woman gave Jane a kind look and handed her the small bouquet of daisies. "Good luck," she said softly.

"Thanks." Jane took the flowers and looked down at the handkerchief. The embroidery wasn't just a design, as she had thought before. In tiny blue, yellow, and pink threads it spelled out the word *Always*. Despite the rush of different emotions she was feeling, Jane realized that she had a new confidence. Maybe it was exhaustion. Maybe the makeover had worked wonders for her, even if Trey hadn't noticed. For the first time in as long as she could remember, she didn't feel cloddishly out of place.

Whatever the reason, she felt strong and steady as she walked to the altar with Trey.

"Do you, Terrence Holden Breckenridge the third, take this woman, Jane Analise Miller, to be your lawfully wedded wife—"

"I do."

The minister shot him a look from her green-lidded eyes and continued, "—to love and to cherish, from this day forward, as long as you both shall live?" She lowered her chin and looked at him expectantly.

This time he hesitated and glanced uncertainly at

Jane, then back at the minister before saying, "I do?"

Evidently this was the right response at the right time because the woman turned to Jane and asked her the same. Not to "obey" he noticed, just to cherish. That was good, because he couldn't see Jane promising to obey someone. Not that it mattered either way.

So why he had this stupid lump in his chest was a mystery to him. Of course he felt affection for Jane. She'd been with him for nearly six years—he'd have to be a robot to feel nothing. Together, they'd been through some really tough times at work and come back. Still, he didn't think his regard for her warranted this kind of excitement. Or was it just plain fear? Maybe it was a little of both.

Or maybe it was just the Mexican food he'd had for dinner. Actually, that seemed a more plausible explanation for the burning in his chest. He'd never been nervous in business before, so why should he start now? This marriage was a simple business maneuver, nothing more. Yet if it was so simple, why was he feeling this boyish anticipation? Why did he feel like this was a real wedding? Should he seriously be contemplating the wedding night, as if they were going to share a bed? No. No way. This was all business.

That's the way Jane was looking at it, so that was the way he was going to look at it too. All business, nothing more.

"May I have the rings now?" Reverend Byrd asked.

"It's, ah, she's already wearing it," Trey said.

The reverend looked at Jane's hand with something like disapproval. "So she is. Not everyone who comes here is that confident in their mate." She turned her saccharine gaze to Trey. "But you still have to say it, honey, 'with this ring, I thee wed'."

He took Jane's hand and said, with a small shrug, "With this ring, I thee wed."

"I now pronounce that you are man and wife." Reverend Byrd beamed appropriately. "You may kiss the bride."

Trey looked at Jane. Her eyes were wide and in her face he saw the same kind of surprise that he was feeling. Aware of the expectations of everyone around them, he moved awkwardly toward Jane and lowered his mouth onto her parted lips.

The touch was charged with all the agitation he'd been feeling for the past ten hours. It buzzed through to his core like an electric shock and felt nearly as dangerous. It also felt good. Damn good.

He wrapped his arms around her and pulled her to him, like a buoy in a stormy sea. Holding her felt safe, it felt good. He could have held her for hours, for days....

"Sixty-seven!"

Chapter Eight

They just barely made the redeye flight back to Dallas. In under five hours, they had flown from Dallas to Las Vegas, gotten married, raced back to the airport and arrived just minutes before the plane was to take off.

As they settled into their seats, the engine hum escalated and within minutes they were taxiing down the runway. Only then did Trey relax a little. He leaned back in his seat, looked around the first-class cabin and noted that it was nearly empty. That was a relief. At this point, he probably wouldn't have been able to breathe if he'd been crowded in by people.

"I need a drink," he said to Jane in a tone that suggested desperation. "How about you?"

"Sure." She pushed her purse under the seat in front of her, just like the flight video instructed. "Ginger ale would be great."

"You sure you don't want something stronger?"

"No, it's okay."

He summoned the steward, and asked, only half-joking, "Is the bar open yet?"

"Certainly, sir." The steward looked from Trey to Jane and back. "Are we celebrating?"

Trey looked at Jane. "I suppose we are, in a way."

"The champagnes are listed—"

"No champagne," Trey interrupted, too gruffly. "That is, not for me." He looked at Jane. "Why don't you have some champagne? A little Dom Perignon? A lot of Dom Perignon?"

She shook her head and looked at the steward. "Ginger ale is fine, thanks."

"I'll have whiskey straight," Trey stated.

The steward went off to get the drinks.

"It's funny but I feel like everyone knows what we just did," Jane said lowly. "Like I look different or like this ring is a great big neon sign. I mean, why would he ask if we were celebrating?"

"Probably because so many people taking the late flight out of Vegas are."

"Oh. I hadn't thought of that. Of course you're right." Her mouth lifted into a wistful smile and he thought again that she was beautiful.

But there was no time for that sort of nonsense. He pulled an address book out of his pocket and lifted the receiver of the telephone in front of him. "You don't happen to have Dick Monroe's number, do you?"

The corners of her mouth went straight. "Not with me now, no."

Why did he suddenly feel so stupid for asking? He replaced the receiver. It wasn't that ridiculous to think his assistant might have her Day-Timer with her, was it? No, it wasn't. It may have been a bit much to expect his bride to have it, but she wasn't his bride, she was his assistant.

In reality—even a new reality that was going way outside familiar territory—that hadn't changed.

The steward brought their drinks and Trey downed his in one burning gulp. "Bring me another one," he said as the man was handing Jane her ginger ale. "Make it two. I don't want to keep you running back and forth all night."

Jane looked concerned. "Do you want something to eat with that?"

He waved the idea away. "I ate this morning."

"But straight whiskey on an empty stomach might not make you feel so hot."

"Don't start getting wifeish on me, Jane." He said it with a smile, but it was a small smile, too stiff to be sincere.

"I wouldn't even know how."

"Good." He cleared his throat. "Let's keep it that way."

She pulled a magazine out of the bag before her and looked at it intently. "Fine."

The steward showed up with the two whiskeys and Trey downed one of them and set the other on the plastic tray. He wasn't normally a drinking man and the whiskey was loosening him up pretty quickly. "And another thing…"

She looked at him. "Yes?"

"We've got to get our roles straight. You're still my secretary."

"Your administrative assistant, right."

"But on paper you're my wife now, too."

"On paper."

The facts were growing somewhat blurry in his own mind. Had he really just married Jane? "But you're really my assistant. So if I ask you to do something, I'm not being a male chauvinist husband, I'm just being your boss. As usual."

"Of course." How did she do that? How did she make those two clipped words make him sound like such an idiot for even bringing it up?

He gave a curt nod and attempted to regain control of the situation. "As long as we're clear on that."

"Absolutely."

He drank some more. "Except we might have to look sometimes like husband and wife instead of like employer and employee. Under certain circumstances."

She laid the magazine in her lap and regarded him. "Under what circumstances?"

"Well..." He thought about that. "Under most circumstances, I guess. Come to think of it, we need the whole outside world to believe that we're really husband and wife so the transfer doesn't come under suspicion."

She nodded. "I see what you mean, but what does really being husband and wife look like? What are you suggesting we do?"

Several answers flew to his mind.

"Is it," she went on, "just things like coming in

together in the morning? Being more informal in our business relationship? Having the same address on legal papers?''

"Yes, things like that." He thought of a few unbusinesslike options, and immediately pushed the thoughts from his mind. "Good. We understand each other."

"Yes. No problem." She returned her full attention to the magazine.

He sank deeper into his chair and nursed his drink. "I wish I'd had time to get you your own ring." He tossed a disapproving glance at Jane's left hand.

She frowned and splayed her fingers. "I don't think I have a choice right now." She tried to pull it again, then sighed. "It won't budge. But it'll probably come off if I use some butter to grease the way."

He took a sip of the whiskey, which was no longer burning because his throat was numb. "I don't know, I just sort of feel like that ring is..." He took a gulp. "Bad luck."

Her brow rose. "Why?"

"It didn't bring my parents any great joy."

Surprise persisted in her eyes. "That wasn't because of the ring."

"I know that." He noticed the puzzlement in her eyes. "You know, it's not that I'm against marriage or anything like that."

She pursed her lips. "It's fine for other people, right?"

"Exactly." He drank. "You know, of all the people who would know that, you'd think my father would be at the top of the list." He drank some more. "He built this business, he knows how consuming it is. Hell, my mother got so lonely she had to leave. Both of us."

A tenderness came into Jane's eyes. "That must have been really difficult for you."

He scoffed. "I was eleven. I was away at school and they'd already separated once before. I guess they figured it wouldn't matter to me anyway."

Her brow lowered. "But it did matter."

He nodded reluctantly. "It mattered." Why was he saying all of this?

"It doesn't have to be that way. Maybe your parents just weren't right for each other and they realized it."

"Forget it." He gave a half-smile. "My point was that Terrence Breckenridge, of all people, should know what a catastrophe marriage is for a man in my position. Yet he pushed anyway. I don't get it."

"Perhaps..." She hesitated and looked uncertain.

"Go on," Trey prompted.

"Perhaps this is what he was talking about when he said all those things about how getting out of the business was the best thing he ever did. Maybe this is exactly why he wanted you married and settled— so you could see how much more fulfilling, in his eyes, family is versus compulsive work. How much more important it is."

Had his father regretted the time lost with his mother? Trey searched his memory. He recalled the funeral, the bright sunshine that seemed to mock the darkness in his heart. Then he recalled his father's face, the deep creases etched into it, the paleness of his skin compared to his black suit. That was the first time Trey had thought his father looked old.

Maybe he had regretted it then. But he hadn't changed his lifestyle for years afterwards. In fact, if anything, he'd worked more.

So that whole theory was out. And it was a good thing too, because it was too depressing to think about.

He took out his address book and credit card again, and reached for the phone. "I've got to call my father and tell him we…did it. Maybe he knows Dick's number."

"Dick can wait until the morning," Jane said, checking her watch. "He knew we were going to do this, so there's no urgency there. I don't think he'd appreciate us calling at this hour to confirm it."

"You're right." Of course she was right. She was always right. "See? This is the sort of thing I need you for. Secretary things, not wife things."

"No wife things," she said softly. "Got it."

With some effort, he punched in the numbers for his father's hotel and told the older man the news. His father regarded it as wonderful, as Trey knew he would. Unlike Dick, he didn't mind being woken up at two a.m. at all.

When he'd finished talking to his father, he hung up the phone, feeling curiously empty. For a moment he'd actually felt excited to relate the news, but then he'd remembered it was all an act and that left him feeling oddly bereft. Then he thought of his mother and an old pain—the heartbreak of an eleven-year-old-boy—shot through him with surprising vitality.

Clearly he needed to relax. He looked at the two empty whiskey glasses and summoned the steward. He needed it. His mind was playing tricks on him. The stress of the day, combined with the sheer exhaustion of everything he'd been through, was making him inappropriately sentimental. He wasn't used to feeling this way and he didn't like it. As soon as he got home, he was going to go straight to bed and sleep for a good twelve hours, at least.

Too bad he had to go to bed alone. He glanced at Jane and let his gaze wander down her slender form.

He ordered another drink and reclined his seat to wait out the rest of the flight.

Jane had never seen Trey drunk before.

Actually, she thought, as she helped him stumble his way onto the elevator in his condominium, probably no one had ever seen him drunk before.

Clearly, he was not used to it.

"Your hair smells good," he said, leaning heavily against her.

"Thanks." She braced herself so he wouldn't fall and reached carefully in front of her to touch the penthouse button. The doors closed with a whoosh and the elevator moved quickly up.

"You always smell good. I noticed that about you."

He didn't seem to be waiting for an answer, which was good because Jane didn't have one.

The elevator stopped and an elderly couple got on and pushed a button.

"I don't know what it is, Jane," he went on, in a hushed tone, "but you've been looking so pretty lately."

She was painfully aware that they weren't alone on the elevator anymore. "I cut my hair," she said lightly.

"Nah, it's not just that." He looked at her and drew a long breath in through his teeth. "It's something...inside. Like a light has been turned on. Maybe it's always been on but I was too busy working to notice it."

Her heart drummed in her ears. She glanced at the couple but they didn't appear to be aware of their conversation. "Maybe."

"But it's definitely on now." He leaned closer to her.

The elevator halted again and the couple moved off.

When they were gone, Trey continued. "What I'm trying to say is that lately I've been having... thoughts..."

Her own breath caught in her chest. "What kind of thoughts?"

"About you...about us..."

She couldn't fall for this. She wouldn't let herself fall for this. It was the whiskey talking, not the man. "'Lately' as in since we got on the plane?"

He shrugged it off and leaned against the wall with a thump. "Did you ever think you'd marry a guy like me?"

"A few times," she admitted, counting on the fact that he wouldn't remember this conversation in the morning.

"I never thought I'd marry a girl like you."

She had no doubt, but still the words stung. "What kind of girl did you think you'd marry?"

"You're too good for me."

She raised her eyebrows. She hadn't expected that. "Is that right?"

"Yep. Way too good. I'm stealing the best year of your life from you. You should hate me."

He really was blind to her. "I don't hate you, Trey."

"You should."

"I don't."

"I do."

She put a hand on his arm. "You shouldn't, Trey."

The doors opened at his suite and he went in without her assistance, though he was slightly wobbly on his feet. "Welcome home," he said, with a broad sweep of his arm and a stumble. "I'd carry you across the threshold but it would almost certainly result in injury. To someone."

"That's okay." Jane walked in and set her bag down at the foot of the stairs. She'd only been here once before and it had been years ago. She'd forgotten how elegant the place was, with its art deco lines and panoramic view of the city outside the back wall of windows. She looked at Trey.

He was already looking at her.

"Would you like me to make you some coffee?"

"My secretary doesn't make coffee." He gave a rakish smile. "Does my wife?"

"Under extreme circumstances." She gave a weak smile and went toward the open kitchen. This was trouble. The alcohol was making him blur lines that shouldn't be blurred. Worse, her foolish heart was all too willing to blur them as well. If she wasn't careful that foolish heart would be broken in no time flat.

Either she or Trey would have to keep their heads tonight, and it obviously was going to have to be her.

He followed her into the kitchen and leaned against the counter. "Then I should have married you years ago."

Keep it light, Jane. He doesn't know what he's saying. He doesn't know what you're hearing. "You never asked." She saw a French coffee press on the counter and took the kettle from the stove to fill it with water.

"What would you have said? If I'd just, out of the blue, asked you to marry me one day?"

She set the kettle on the stove and turned the burner on high. "Apparently I would have said yes, since you did ask me out of the blue one day."

"No, no, no, you know what I mean. If it were not under duress. If I'd just waltzed in and said, 'Jane, will you marry me?'"

Her heart was pounding madly. "Where do you keep the coffee?"

"In the freezer." He gave a vague gesture in that direction. "What would you have said if I'd done that?"

"It depends on why you would have done it," she answered carefully.

He smiled again. He really could have been a movie star. "To sleep with you, of course."

A tingle ran down her spine but she kept focused on her task, rinsing out the coffee press with great care. "How could I resist such honorable motives?"

"Hey." He moved across the kitchen floor and put his hands on her shoulders. Her tense shoulders melted under his touch. "At least I was honest. That's honorable."

"Theoretically honest, you mean."

"Eh?"

Why had she encouraged this? "Forget it." She moved to the freezer, forcing his arms to drop to his sides. She took the coffee out and scooped some of the fragrant grounds into the press. "Strong?"

"Very strong."

Her hand was shaking as she put another scoop in.

He came up behind her and said, into her ear, "What if I married you and then said I wanted to sleep with you?"

She longed to lean back into him, but instead she busied herself with pouring the boiling water over the coffee grounds and replacing the top. "Then I'd have to commend your honesty again."

"And what would your answer be?" He flashed a devilish smile. "Theoretically, that is."

She gave her best nonchalant look. "I would probably have to point out that you've had a little too much to drink and you're not quite yourself."

"Meaning you don't believe this is a sincere desire?" He touched his finger lightly to her hair and watched her for her answer.

"It may be a sincere desire, at the moment, but that doesn't mean it's a good idea for us to follow through with it." *Tomorrow you may consider it a sincere regret. If you remember at all.*

"What would make it a good idea?" He trailed his hands along her ribs and tantalizingly low across her abdomen. "Tell me. I'll do anything."

She couldn't help it, she relaxed against him. "This is a bad idea."

He reached across her hips and turned her to face him. "That's what they said to Orville and Wilbur." He lowered his mouth onto hers.

"We're not flying," she said when his lips were just inches away from her own.

"We could be." He kissed her deeply. The light scent of whiskey was fiercely masculine. She found it more intoxicating than the drink itself. His powerful arms closed around her, making her feel improbably delicate within their embrace.

As his mouth moved against hers, lulling her into submission, he trailed his finger gently down her cheek, then cupped his hands behind her head, holding her gently as he kissed away her objections. There was nothing clumsy or drunken about his moves now.

She sank into him, trying to stop herself but knowing she was powerless against her own desire. She wanted this like she'd never wanted anything before in her life. "Are you sure we should be doing this?" she asked stupidly.

"It's the only thing I've been sure of all day."

"What if you regret it tomorrow?"

He stopped and pulled back. "Are you saying you'll regret it?"

Not this again. "No," she said. "No, I'm not."

"Then we agree." He kissed her again. He moved his hands lightly down her ribs and to the zipper in the back of her dress. He unzipped it slowly, working his mouth against hers in the most sensual way.

The zipper stuck halfway.

"What's wrong?" she asked breathlessly, feeling it stop.

"It's stuck."

"Stuck?" Her heart sank. It was "A Sign."

He laughed. Apparently he wasn't worried about signs from above. "Seems to be."

"This is a bad omen."

He cupped his hands around her face. "I don't believe in omens." Then he kissed her.

"Give me just a minute," she said, pulling back. "I want to change my clothes." *I want to regain my senses. I want to be able to breathe again. I have to talk myself out of this.* "I'll be right back."

He leveled his gaze at her. "Let me help you out of it," he said with a pirate smile. "I'll buy you a new dress. I'll buy you ten new dresses."

She felt the flush in her cheeks. "I'll just be a minute. You have some coffee."

"I don't want coffee, I want you." He pulled her into a dizzying kiss again.

A huge part of her wanted to stay and give him just that, but she knew she had to collect herself first.

She drew back from the embrace. "Trey, I'll be back." She disentangled herself from his arms and went back to the foyer, where she'd left her bag.

She took it into the spacious marble powder room on the main floor and closed the door behind her. The minute she was alone, she dropped her bag onto the closed commode and went to the sink. When she saw her reflection in the mirror—the hopeful eyes, the lips, flushed from kissing—she sighed heavily. Things were happening too fast.

She splashed her face with the coldest water she could get from the tap and looked at herself again. The hope was still there. She could see it in her face as clearly as she could feel it in her soul.

With great purpose, she opened her bag and looked at her options. She only had about three other outfits with her, and that was thanks to Peatie. She'd also tossed in a long cotton night shirt, but that was obviously out of the question.

She tried on two of the outfits but they were for work and she would have looked idiotic coming out in one of them. The third was also for work but it was much more casual, slender black pants and a soft grey shirt.

Next, she dug through her purse for the few cosmetics she had. Peatie had given her simple instructions for using them, and she had to admit they highlighted her features pretty effectively.

Finally, she tackled her hair. It had been a long day and her hair was limp and lifeless. She pulled it back into a casual chignon, and looked in the mirror. Too grannyish. She put it in a top knot. Too girlish.

Eventually she just brushed it back away from her face where it fell in gentle waves.

She was finished. There was nothing else to keep her from going back out to Trey. Somehow she had hoped she might gain clarity by getting away from him for a few minutes, but nothing had changed. It was already clear in her mind that she shouldn't become intimate with Trey in this condition. But her heart was yearning for it, regardless of the circumstances, as much as ever. Maybe even more.

With no alternative plan, she decided she'd go back to Trey and play it by ear. Perhaps a plan that hadn't come to her while she was alone would come to her when she was with him.

He was no longer in the kitchen where she'd left him. Soft music hummed in the living room. Louis Armstrong and Ella Fitzgerald were singing "Let's Face the Music and Dance." That seemed to be the order of the night.

Trey was sitting on the couch. Though her legs were trembling, Jane forced herself to walk into the room with confidence.

"Sorry I took so long," she began, but he didn't budge. She rounded the corner and saw why. He was sitting there, coffee in hand, sound asleep.

"Oh, Trey." She smiled sadly. Of course this was for the best, but part of her was aching for him. "Come on, let's get you comfortable at least." She took the cup from his hand and set it on the coffee table.

He roused slightly. "What?"

"Lie down and sleep it off." She helped ease him onto his back.

"Jane?" he mumbled very softly. "I was just thinking about you."

She took a cotton throw from the back of the couch and draped it over him. "Funny, I was just thinking about you, too."

"I wonder if we were thinking the same thing."

"Probably." She bent to smooth the blanket.

He took her upper arm in his hand. "Stay with me." His grip loosened and his hand trailed down her arm, falling heavily at his side. He was out again.

Stay with me. She touched his face, ran her hand across his hair. "I wish I could," she whispered. "I'd stay with you forever if you wanted me too." She kissed his cheek.

With one last lingering look at him, his face smooth and untroubled in sleep, she turned off the light and went to find a guest room.

Chapter Nine

What had he *done?*

Trey woke up feeling like he was wearing a mashed-potato helmet, and craving water like a man in the desert. He stood up unsteadily. It took him a moment to get his bearings and another minute to figure out where he was. He was in the living room. Why was he in the living room? It wasn't easy for his throbbing brain to compute, but he remembered. He'd slept on the couch. He put a hand to his aching lower back. He was too old to sleep on the couch.

More specifically, he was too old to be passing out on the couch.

He made his way through the early morning light to the kitchen and filled a big glass of water from the tap. He drank lustily, then refilled the glass and took the aspirin out of the cabinet. He shook out two tablets, remembered Las Vegas the night before, and shook out one more.

He had married Jane Miller.

But that wasn't all he remembered. He had wanted her, almost desperately, last night. Quiet, competent Jane had turned into sexy, alluring, arousing Jane and he'd wanted her desperately. Jane! His head throbbed anew at the implications.

What had he done?

He almost didn't want to remember the details. Jane was probably horrified. After years of her painfully perfect etiquette in the office, he had rewarded her by leering and hanging all over her. He'd probably even drooled.

He stopped. Come to think of it, where was Jane? Maybe he'd offended her so much she'd left. Maybe she'd even dissolved the marriage already. If anyone could have found out where and how to get a quickie divorce between midnight and—he checked his watch—six a.m., it would be her.

He sat on a barstool in the kitchen, put his elbows on the counter and hung his head in his hands. She wouldn't have done that, she wouldn't have undone everything they'd gone through yesterday. She was too kind to let Rankin put the screws to him, even if he had offended her to the core. Somehow he'd have to make it up to her.

If only he could remember everything that had happened.

While Trey was sifting through the foggy details in his mind, Jane came downstairs and into the kitchen. He didn't know she was there until the light flashed on like an unexpected blast of noise. He jerked to attention. She looked pale and wide-eyed, holding a hand to her chest. Obviously she was as surprised to see him as he was to see her.

"Sorry, I—"

He held up a hand. "It's all right. Not your fault."

"I was just going to make a little coffee and go into the office," she said, sounding like a guilty teenager.

What did she have to feel guilty about? He was the one who'd committed all the offenses. "It's too early to go into the office." You were hoping to avoid me, weren't you?

"I couldn't sleep, so I figured I may as well."

"Funny, I was thinking the same thing."

Silence hung between them.

"We have a lot to do today," Jane ventured, with a dismissive wave of her hand.

"That's true." He was all too conscious of the fact that the conversation was meaningless. It wasn't what they said to each other, it was what they weren't saying. He had to broach the subject. "Look, I'm really sorry about coming on to you that way last night."

A faint smile touched her lips. That was good. At least, it was better than the mortification she'd expected. "I'm surprised you remember."

"I remember enough. I think," he added with new uncertainty. "Anyway, I remember more than I want to." He raked his hand across his hair. "I feel just awful about it."

She didn't look at him. Perhaps it was worse than he thought. "Forget it, Trey." She kept her eyes focused on the floor. "It wasn't that big a deal."

He looked for some way to reassure her. "It's not like I've been secretly lusting after you for years and finally made my move, so to speak."

"Of course not." Her voice was clipped.

"I really want you to know that. It was a one-time thing. I was drunk. Really drunk. You don't have to worry that I'll ever do it again." He had to remember that and never, ever try anything with her again, because, looking at her now, he realized that his feelings the night before hadn't been an aberration. She was tempting, even first thing in the morning when he was suffering from a whopper of a hangover.

"I'm not sure what was wrong with me last night," he tried again, but he didn't sound like he meant it. "I won't even try to make excuses for it. But I want to assure you that I'll never do anything like that again."

She turned to face him and he could have sworn there were tears in her big, luminous eyes. Under other circumstances, his pride might have been injured upon realizing a woman was upset to the point of tears because he'd tried to make love to her. Under these circumstances, though, he was terrified that he had driven her out of his life.

"Can we please not talk about this anymore?" she asked. "You've made it really clear that nothing like that will ever happen again, and that it was all some big moment of insanity on your part. I've got it. Let's just drop it, okay?"

That stung. It wasn't like Jane to be so curt with him. But heaven knew he deserved it. "Just wanted to get it all out in the open."

"It's out there." She looked to an empty spot in the middle of the room, then to Trey. "I think I'll just stop for coffee on my way in. Would you excuse me?" She didn't wait for an answer, but turned and left the room.

He wanted to stop her but he didn't trust himself. "Of course," he called after her. "I'll see you there."

"Fine." Without looking back, she grabbed her bag and went out the door.

Trey gazed at the door for several seconds after she'd gone. There was an uncomfortable tightness in his chest. Stress. Maybe even a heart attack. He should probably see a doctor, but he wasn't going to. He turned his focus toward the day ahead and his tension increased. Definitely stress. And getting married wasn't the end of it. He still had to sign his assets—his life—over to Jane.

He could have kicked himself for taking such a foolish chance on alienating the most important person in his life. Without her, he was ruined.

Hastily, he started a pot of coffee. He should get in to the office early, too. The sooner he started the paperwork, the sooner he'd finish and get on with his life.

Whatever that meant now.

When Jane got to the office, she closed the door behind her and leaned against it, reveling in a moment of feeling normal. Every day for nearly six years she'd been the first one in. She walked through her morning routine, breathing deeply to try and ease her thundering heart. She turned on the lights, and immediately remembered doing the same thing in Trey's kitchen an hour earlier. With impatience and embarrassment she remembered the momentary thrill she'd felt at seeing him there. *Would he remember?* she'd asked herself hopefully. *Would he sweep her into his arms and take up where he'd left off the night before?*

The idea that he would be so embarrassed about it, that he would tell her straight out that he'd never had feelings for her and that it was all the result of drinking too much, hadn't even crossed her mind. Which was strange, because usually she was all too ready to believe exactly that sort of thing.

Yet last night her deepest instincts had told her that when he'd kissed her, he'd meant it. Foolish instincts. She wouldn't be trusting them again.

She stopped in the copy-room and turned on the photocopiers. Her heart felt heavy. Countless times she'd stopped in this same room in the morning, wondering, as she clicked the machines on one by one, if this would be the day that Trey would finally notice her. Now she longed for those days of blissful ignorance.

As she rounded the corner toward her office, a deep floral scent hit her. When she went into her office, she couldn't believe her eyes. There was a bouquet of at least three-dozen red roses on her desk. Her heart leapt foolishly and she rushed to open the card.

To the new Mrs. Breckenridge,
Welcome to the family. Here's to the many happy years to come!

With love from Terrence

Well, what had she been hoping for?

She'd been hoping that, even though it was impossible for him to have sent them, they were from Trey. She'd been hoping that the card said something personal, something affectionate, something to feed her hope. She sat down and took a moment to collect her thoughts. Silence pounded around her. It was impossible to escape her own hopes.

Mrs. Breckenridge.
Welcome to the family.
Many happy years.

When she'd agreed to this marriage—was it only yesterday?—she'd known it was all business. Nothing was different now, so why was her heart breaking? Certainly the flowers and the card were poignant reminders that this wasn't real, but they were only reminders. Nothing had changed.

She ripped the card in half and tried to toss it into the trash but couldn't bear to. Terrence's heart was in that gesture, she couldn't just toss it away. Instead she tucked it into the back of a drawer.

She sat for a long time, lost in thought. By the time the phone shrilled, startling her out of her self-pity, the office outside her door was humming with the activity of a new day.

She pressed the line button and answered the phone. It was Peatie.

"I knew you'd be there. Did you do it?"

Jane lowered her head into her hands. She felt like crying as soon as she heard the familiar voice of her friend. "We did it all right."

"You don't sound happy."

"What's to be happy about?"

"You're Trey's wife!"

Jane paused. "No, I'm not. I'm just the person he married. It's not very different than anything else I do here—I sign his letters, see clients for him, juggle his schedule."

A sigh of utter frustration crackled across the line. "I take it things didn't go well with the wedding night."

"It wasn't a wedding night in any real sense," Jane began. As if on cue, the outside office door creaked open and slammed shut. Jane recognized Trey's absent whistle echoing through the halls.

"What was it then?" Peatie was asking.

Jane bit her lower lip. "Peatie, I can't talk right now. He just walked in."

She hung up the phone as Trey walked into the room. Was it her imagination or did his face color slightly when he saw her?

"Hello," he said, as if they hadn't seen each other already this morning.

"Hello," she said, in exactly the same way.

He took his jacket off. "Could you get Dick Monroe on the phone for me?"

"Sure." She flipped through her phone file to Monroe, and lifted the receiver.

"Wait—Jane."

She looked up. "Yes?"

"I—" He shook his head. "Never mind."

"All right." She watched him turn and go into his office, wondering what it was he'd almost said. Jane had never put much faith in psychic premonition, but something inside of her was telling her that it was important.

It was the same part of her that wouldn't quite accept the idea that she should give up on Trey. After all, he had kissed her, he'd held her. That kind of thing didn't come from nowhere. Especially not from a man like Trey. In his position he wasn't the kind of man who could afford to follow foolish momentary whims like that.

Jane sighed. Her logical mind still insisted that she forget about him. After all, he'd said, plain as anything, that he'd never had feelings for her and that kissing her had been a mistake. She should believe him.

But in her heart she didn't. Not quite.

The kind of confidence that went into hanging on to that hope was uncharacteristic for Jane. It was a change she hadn't expected when she and Peatie were revamping her hair and clothes and makeup. Somehow, maybe during that process, Jane had begun to change inside. She liked it.

Two nights later, Trey needed Jane to play wife for a new audience.

"Luigi Bonatelli is coming to dinner?" Jane repeated. "For a home-cooked Italian dinner? Why?"

"Because he hasn't had a home-cooked Italian dinner since his wife died three years ago," Trey told her, with a mixture of excitement and trepidation. "Coincidentally, the very reason he's looking to sell his construction supply company and move back to the homeland."

Jane frowned. "And you're thinking of buying it? Now? When we're not even sure we can keep Breckenridge afloat?"

He stiffened at the truth. "Breckenridge Construction is going to be fine. More than fine, we're going to prosper, with just this kind of diversification."

"But how are you going to pay for it?"

"Are you forgetting Davenport?"

She looked down and he knew in an instant that she hadn't forgotten Davenport but she'd written it off as a failed deal. He couldn't allow himself to think the same thing, as tempting as it was. He had to believe it would come through. "Owning the equipment supply company that every other construction firm turns to is going to give us a huge advantage," he finished, impressing even himself with his confidence. "But the problem is, he won't sell to just anyone."

"So you figure if we do the personal family bit, he'll warm to the idea of selling to you."

Trey was momentarily stunned. "Right again, Watson."

A hint of a smile suggested itself in her eyes. "You don't think the act is wearing a little thin?"

"Are you kidding? This is the best hook I've ever used." He was smiling broadly, to show he wasn't such a bad guy as this truth made him sound. "I should have tried it years ago."

Jane smiled, glanced at the clock, then sighed and sat down at her desk and wearily took out a pen and paper. "If I hurry I can get to the store in ten minutes and be home to start the lasagna in forty-five. What time is he coming?"

"Seven, but you don't have to cook." What if she couldn't cook? What if she insisted on doing it herself and it was lousy? After all, he couldn't expect her to be able to do everything.

"I don't?"

He made a face. "Nah, just pick something up at Tony's."

"That's not quite homemade."

"Close enough. It's good."

Jane persisted. "But you said you wanted to give him a home-made Italian dinner."

"So we'll heat it up at home."

"Trey—"

He held up a hand. "Jane, seriously. There isn't time to make a big spread from scratch."

She narrowed her eyes. "You think I'll make a bad dinner and ruin it for you."

"I didn't say that—"

She laughed. "You didn't have to. Trust me, Trey."

He looked at her. Trust her. She'd never let him down before, but was that any reason to tempt fate this way?

She waited, watching him steadily, waiting for his answer.

"I trust you," he said at last, and meant it.

"Good." She stood up and shoved the grocery list she'd jotted down into her purse. "I'm going."

"Okay." He smiled. "I'm going with you."

Jane was a marvel in the grocery store, choosing the best vegetables, the most fragrant herbs, the leanest cuts of meat. Trey had never had any idea that there were so many variables. Yet Jane moved along with the confidence of one who has spent her life studying the firmness of tomatoes and the difference between sweet basil and purple-leaf basil.

He'd never had so much fun at the grocery store before. The fact that it could be fun at the grocery store at all was surprising, but he was even more surprised at how much he was enjoying just being with Jane, doing ordinary things.

She was no less amazing at home in the kitchen, though it was a little less fun when she swatted him with the dishtowel every time he tried to taste the sauce.

"It's not ready yet," she said, moving to the refrigerator. He noted the sway of her hips as she moved and thought, not for the first time, how graceful and feminine her stature was.

She took two carrots out of the refrigerator and began grating them into the bubbling tomato sauce on the stove. "This is the most important part."

"Carrot?" He shifted his thoughts from her form

to her cooking. "You're putting that into spaghetti sauce?"

She paused over the grater and looked at him with luminous, wide eyes. "Are you saying Mama Massi is wrong?"

"Who's Mama Massi?"

She lifted her brow as if to say are you joking? and resumed grating. "Mama Massi," she said with a smile, "was the old widow who lived across the street from my family when I was growing up. She assured me for years that she would someday tell me the secret to her lasagna. It was the hit of every funeral and hospital recuperation in the neighborhood, you know." She smiled again, set the grater aside, and stirred the sauce with a wooden spoon. "Anyway, finally, when she was almost ninety or so, she called me over, I'll never forget it, and she said to me, 'Jane, *cara mia,* I don't have much longer on this earth. I tell you the secret of my sauce.'"

Trey's heart pounded at the humorous gleam in Jane's eye. "You're making this up," he said.

She sobered immediately. "I'm not, I swear it. That's exactly what she said, then she told me you grate two carrots into a pot of sauce and let it cook slowly, over two days, releasing its sweetness into the sauce."

"Two days?"

Jane shrugged and took a lid out of the cabinet. "I know. That would be ideal. I'm going to have to hurry it along with the pressure cooker." She secured the lid on and turned the heat on the stove up to high.

He watched this operation, stealing a taste of garlicky pesto sauce when Jane turned her back. It was delicious. ''What happened to Mama Massi?''

''Mmm?'' She glanced at the pesto, then at Trey, with a suspicious look. She dipped her finger into the pesto and held it out to Trey. ''Try this.''

He hesitated.

''Go on,'' she said, moving her hand toward him.

He caught her by the wrist and slowly tasted the pesto from her finger. Their eyes locked for a moment and he held her hand there.

Then they both suddenly laughed. It was the strangest reaction.

''Very good,'' Trey said, nodding appreciatively.

''You don't think there's too much garlic?''

''Nope.''

''I used walnuts instead of pine nuts. You think that's okay?''

He nodded. ''It's perfect.'' *You're perfect.* ''So what ever happened to Mama Massi?''

Jane wiped her hands hastily on her apron. ''Oh, Mama Massi went on for another six years, protesting all along that she was on her deathbed. She was quite a character.''

She was a character, he thought. And in Jane's retelling, she was bringing a warmth to his home that he'd never even realized was lacking.

He'd told Jane he didn't want her for wifely duties, only secretarial. He didn't need a wife, he'd said belligerently, and he didn't want one.

Now he wasn't so sure.

Luigi Bonatelli proclaimed the dinner ''Exquisite,'' the company, ''charming,'' and the evening on the whole ''a delight.''

In fact, Trey and Jane created what she had called the "cosy, homey atmosphere" so convincingly that Trey himself had begun to fall for it. As the evening wore on, with Jane delivering one delicious course after another to the table, he found himself taking more pride in her than in himself.

It wasn't that he was relying on her to win his case for him—he already knew enough about Bonatelli's passions to win him over to the deal. The surprising thing was that he realized that he didn't want to prevent Jane's own star from shining.

If that was even possible, which he doubted.

"You know, Trey," Luigi said, swabbing a large dab of cannoli cream from the corner of his mouth at the end of the meal, "this woman cooks so well she could almost pass for an Italian."

"She does everything well," Trey murmured, then said, "She's a wonder, I have to agree."

"You know," Luigi went on, pouring cream into his coffee with gusto. "You can tell a lot about a man's judgment by the wife he picks for himself."

Hadn't his father said almost exactly the same thing?

"Interesting," Luigi continued, "since you can tell almost nothing about a woman from her choice of men." He gave an easy laugh. "We're all unworthy."

Trey nodded. "Fortunately, we don't have much competition."

"Speaking of competition," Jane said, steering the

conversation artfully. "Trey tells me you have people lining up with the hopes of buying your company before you return to Sicily."

Sicily? Trey jerked his head toward her. How did she know that?

"Ah." Luigi waved a hand airily. "If your husband wants the company it's his. It's obvious to me that this is a man who cares about heart."

Trey looked from Luigi to Jane and back again. "That's it? You'll sell?"

"Mmm." The other man nodded, then his face broke into a smile. "That is, assuming we agree on a price."

"I'm sure we can," Trey said, looking at Jane with amazement. This had been too easy. It had been too fun. The work had been more enjoyable than the payoff.

That was strange.

Jane gave Trey a barely perceptible nod of congratulations. "Luigi, you must tell us about your father. Wasn't he the first Bonatelli to come to the United States?"

With that, Luigi was off and running. So was Breckenridge Construction, for that matter. Things couldn't have gone more smoothly. The best part of it was that everything Luigi had enjoyed and appreciated about the evening, Trey had enjoyed and appreciated too.

There had been none of the nervousness and self-consciousness that had gone with his and Jane's first evening out with his father. Things were easing into a natural swing, almost as though they were really, well, a couple.

This was dangerous.

Later that night, as they were sharing a nightcap and discussing the evening, Trey found himself feeling more and more drawn to Jane. "I could get used to this," he heard himself say.

"Get used to what?"

It was on the tip of his tongue to say, "To being married," but he stopped himself. That would be a mistake. He couldn't get used to being married, he wasn't the marrying kind. This was infatuation. Physical lust, pure and simple.

If he was foolish enough to suggest to Jane that they make the arrangement permanent, it would be the biggest mistake of his life. They'd both end up sorry for it.

"Get used to what, Trey?" she repeated.

"To," he searched for the answer, and tried to ignore the dreamy question in her eyes, "to buying different kinds of companies."

"Oh." Her face fell. "You do seem to have a knack for it."

He nodded briskly. "Let's just hope it goes through. You know, I'm pretty sick of having everything depending on Davenport to come through. That check better arrive this week."

"I'm sure it will," she said, in a hollow voice. When she looked at him, he noticed that a spark that had been in her eyes all evening had been extinguished.

He had extinguished it.

His nerves immediately tightened. What could he do? Lead her on? Make love to her and make her believe there was more to the marriage than there was?

He couldn't do that to her. He may be hurting her now, but it was nothing compared to the hurt she'd feel after that kind of betrayal. Jane Miller wasn't the kind of woman you used in the heat of passion. She wasn't the kind of woman you just had sex with, then set aside.

Jane Miller was the kind of woman you married.

That was the problem. In marrying her, he had used her as surely as if he'd used her for sex. He couldn't lead her on—hell, he couldn't lead them both on—anymore. They'd done enough of the cosy, homey act.

Now it was back to business. And as soon as the check came from Davenport and the debt to Rankin was cleared, it was back to bachelorhood.

Over the next week, no payment came from Davenport. Every day things became more and more tense around Breckenridge Construction and around Trey. At work, he was constantly on edge, and he was constantly at work. Jane didn't run into him at the apartment even once. Under other circumstances, she would have thought he was avoiding her, but the financial picture was so dismal that even she couldn't imagine he was doing anything other than staying at the office, fretting and trying to find a way out of an increasingly impossible situation.

Rankin had called the loan, exactly as expected.

Ironically, Trey's one moment of levity had occurred when Dick Monroe had described the shock of Rankin's attorney when he was informed that Trey had no assets. Trey, Jane, and Dick had gotten a bit of a stiff laugh out of that, but Trey had fallen quiet after a few moments and his demeanor had been pensive ever since.

The suit was going forward, with Rankin and his team scrambling to find a way to get at the assets through Jane, but for the time being Trey and the company were safe.

After six days of excruciating waiting, a registered letter came from Davenport. Jane signed for it but hesitated before taking it in to Trey. The envelope was small, and too thin to contain the ratified contract they were expecting.

She held the envelope up to the light. She recognized the Davenport logo on the paper within but couldn't read the jumble of words on the folded papers. She lowered it to the desk. What was she trying to do? It wasn't as if she could protect Trey from the contents by knowing them in advance.

With great trepidation, she got up, went to his office and tapped lightly on the door. "Trey?"

"Come on in, Jane."

She opened the door and stepped in, closing it discreetly behind her.

Trey observed her, then said, "This doesn't look like good news."

"I don't know what it is." She held the envelope out to him.

He took it and, just as Jane had, held it up to the

light. "Doesn't look like the contract to me," he said curtly.

"Call me if you need anything," Jane said, and turned to go.

"Jane."

She turned back. "Yes?"

"I need you."

Her heart thrummed. "What can I do?"

"We'll know in a minute." He tore the envelope open. "Whatever is in here is going to require some sort of action, I can guarantee you that."

She waited as he took the single sheet of paper out and read it. It seemed to take an eternity before he finally clicked his tongue against his teeth and leaned back in his chair, letting the paper flutter to the desk.

"What did it say?" Jane asked.

"They're canceling the contract."

"What?" She had imagined the letter had detailed problems, or changes to the terms, but not cancellation. "The whole thing is off?"

"The whole thing is off."

"But—but…why?"

He gestured impatiently at the letter. "You can read it. Basically it says that the terms weren't what they expected, the numbers didn't match theirs, etc. etc. etc., but what it means is that they've changed their minds about us and they want out."

"That doesn't make sense. Our bid was fair, our work is excellent, and nothing has changed since we agreed on the terms in the first place."

When Trey answered, his voice was deadly calm. "One thing has changed."

"What?" Jane was beginning to feel worried.

"Since we bid on this deal, the president of Breckenridge Construction has had financial troubles and transferred his assets to his wife. His new wife." He thumped his palm against the side of his head. "It's so stupid. I can't believe I didn't think of this. I was so busy trying to prevent legal action that it never even occurred to me how this would look to the companies we do business with."

Without stopping to censor her moves, Jane went around the desk and laid a hand on his shoulder from behind. "Trey, there's no reason you should have been concerned with that. How would anyone find out about it? Come to think of it, how did Davenport find out about it?"

Trey turned his chair to face her. "I can only think of one way. Rankin put them on to it."

Jane started to object, then stopped and thought about it. "As a stockholder here, Rankin would have a lot to lose by sabotaging the deal."

Trey nodded. "It's a drop in the bucket for him. If his drive for revenge is as great as my dad thinks it is, he can afford it."

"You honestly think he'd let the whole company go under, just so he can exact revenge on you?"

He gave a humorless spike of laughter. "Maybe. Or maybe he thinks he can get control of the company and stop it from going completely bankrupt." He threw his hands up. "I have no idea what he's thinking."

She shifted her weight. "Actually, there's no way to be sure that Rankin is behind this."

"I've been in business long enough to trust my instincts in cases like this. Rankin's behind it." There was no doubt in his voice at all.

"Well, however this happened, we can't give up."

A moment passed, then Trey looked at her as if he had only just heard her. "What did you say?"

"I said we're not going to give up. We have to fight back."

His eyes softened and only then did she notice just how haggard he looked. The smile lines she loved were deep creases, and there were dark circles under his eyes. "With all this, you're not going to cut your losses and get out?"

"What, and leave you here to deal with all of this alone? Not on your life."

He reached for her hand and pulled her one step closer to him. "You're one in a million."

"So are you," she said softly.

"I don't deserve you." He kissed her palm, then looked up into her eyes, still holding her hand. "But if you're willing to stay, I'm sure as hell going to keep you."

She gathered her nerve. "Are you still talking about business?"

He raised an eyebrow. "How much are you willing to let me have?"

"All of me." The words were out before she could stop herself. But it was okay because she didn't want to stop herself. Not anymore.

In one swift move, he pulled her onto his lap and

circled his arms around her. "Are you sure about that?"

She felt strong in his embrace. "I'm sure."

He pushed her hair back off her face, tenderly trailing his fingertip along her temple. "You're so pretty."

She felt her face grow hot and looked down. "Thanks," she said, with a small laugh.

He remained serious. "I mean it." He cupped his hand on her cheek. "You're not easy to resist."

"Why resist?" A feeling of unreality swirled in her mind as she spoke the words that were so unlike her. But it felt so good.

"Because if we go where I'd like to go, things won't be the same anymore." He laughed suddenly. "It could ruin our marriage."

She smiled and hoped that he couldn't hear the eager thrumming of her heart. "I'm willing to take that chance." Could this dream really come true?

He pulled her toward him and kissed her lightly on the lips then drew back slightly. For just a moment he looked into her eyes, their breath mingling before them. Then with a slight shake of his head he gave into his desire and kissed her again, this time with hunger.

Her heart pounded so hard that she grew dizzy, spiraling into a dreamy wonderland, full of colors and music and sensations she couldn't even name.

She was barely aware of her surroundings, but the sound of laughter down the hall caught part of her attention. "The door," Jane murmured through the haze, wondering if this was a dream. "It's not locked."

"I don't care."

"I do." She pulled back, breathless. "Let me lock it." This answered the question of whether or not this was a dream. It had to be real. In her dreams she was never so practical.

Trey put a hand on her arm. "Last time you left me in this condition you didn't come back."

So he remembered. "I'm going ten feet away." She turned the lock, still feeling so lightheaded she had to lean against the door to catch her breath. "See?"

He stood up and met her in the middle of the room. Wordlessly, he took her into his arms and kissed her again, pulling her against him until she felt herself melt into him. There was no separation between them.

"I want you, Jane," he whispered.

She nearly cried out at hearing the words she'd fantasized of for so long.

"I think I've wanted you for a long time," he went on. "Tell me you feel the same way."

"I do," she whispered softly. "I do." She was afraid if she spoke, it might break this fragile illusion.

"Are you sure?" He moved his hand down her back and rested it on her hip. She tingled beneath the slight weight of his touch.

"More sure than I've ever been." She reached for his hand and, with trembling anticipation, guided it to the front of her pants. The heat of his flesh on the other side of the thin material was exciting. "No doubts."

"It feels like I've waited forever for this." Taking his time, he lowered her pants off over her hips, watching her eyes. Every time his fingers grazed her skin, she shuddered with pleasure.

"So do I." Nervously, she brought her hand to the button on his pants and fumbled to open it. Her need grew with an urgency that surprised her. He helped her, without making her feel embarrassed, and kicked off the pants. She expected to feel shy, but she didn't. She felt completely comfortable with him.

She knew this was right.

He drew back and, without bothering with the buttons, pulled his shirt off with one tug. Now was not the time for timidity, Jane decided, laying her hands to his chest in the way she'd imagined hundreds of times. It was even stronger and harder than she'd imagined. He was a powerful man, physically, and she shook with the anticipation of feeling him inside of her.

She'd wanted this for so long, it was hard to believe that it was all happening now.

Wordlessly, she allowed him to slowly unbutton her blouse, each button bringing her closer to the union she craved. When her shirt was on the floor, he took his time, caressing her, trailing his hand across her skin. Kissing her senses into oblivion, he unhooked her bra and slipped it off. It dropped onto the growing pile of clothes on the floor. Finally, he slid her panties over her hips. She trembled as he knelt before her and extended his hand up to her.

It made her heart constrict to look at him. He wanted her. He was asking for her, for her, not for anyone else.

She took his hand, and knelt in front of him, shaking so strongly inside that she doubted she could have stood much longer. He smiled, the very smile she'd loved for so long, and her heart nearly stopped. Then he pulled her into his arms again.

From there, Jane surrendered completely to the ache she had felt for five years. It was even better than she could have imagined, and she'd imagined it plenty of times. Tenderly, slowly, he introduced her to the physical pleasures she had never known but had long wondered about. She knew, even as he took her, that she would never regret relinquishing her virginity to him. He was the only man she had ever truly loved.

Afterward, they lay locked in each others arms on the floor. "You should have told me it was your first time," he chided her huskily.

She felt her face grow warm and hurriedly glanced at the floor. "Was it that obvious?" She couldn't see anything that would make it obvious.

He kissed her cheek. "Not in the way you're thinking. You were wonderful. Incredible."

Her embarrassment turned to a flush of pleasure. "I wasn't asking for praise. But thanks."

"These surroundings are seriously unworthy." He gestured at the desk. "We should have been in some fancy hotel room, with gilded walls and satin sheets with rose petals strewn across the bed. Or something."

"I'm perfectly happy with the way it was, thank you very much." He would never know just how much she meant it, but that was okay. This was one happiness that she could keep in her heart forever, to take out and look at whenever she wanted to.

He looked at her. "You deserve the best." He touched her lips. "I wish I could give it to you. Unfortunately, I'll probably be living in this office before long."

"Trey, don't talk that way. It's not true."

"That's right, it's not. We're going to fight."

"Exactly."

He chuckled softly. "I can't tell you what it meant to hear you say that. I've never met a woman who would accept me for who I was, no matter what the circumstances."

"For better or worse," Jane said, then realized the irony. "So to speak."

He looked at her oddly for a moment, then nodded. "So to speak."

They lay in silence for a few moments, then Jane said, "We should probably get back to work. There's a lot that needs to be done."

"It can wait," Trey groaned. "This is the most relaxed I've been in months. I don't want it to end."

"I don't either."

"But you're right. There's a lot to do." He made no move to get up.

She didn't either. "Tons."

"This is a place of business, after all." His tone was lazy. "We should be working here." He tightened his arm around her.

"Absolutely."

"Somehow I like what we did better."

"Me too." She paused uncertainly. "So, seriously, it was really…okay?"

He pretended not to know what she was talking about. "Was what okay?"

She rolled her eyes heavenward. "The dictation I took earlier."

"Ah, the dictation." He smiled mischievously. "I think it was okay."

That smile was one that never failed to melt her. "You think so?"

He nodded. "But we may have to do it again." He pulled her close and kissed her face, her ear, and her neck. "Just to be sure."

He kissed her deeply, nudging his tongue against hers, and working it artfully to inflame her arousal. Her body came alive with anticipation, as she wrapped her arms around him and surrendered, once again, to her desire.

Chapter Ten

It was just after 2:00 p.m. when Trey fell asleep on the couch in his office. They had spent hours together, ignoring the rest of the world as it churned by. It had been restorative for both of them. Clearly for Trey, it had been a tremendous release. Jane watched him for several minutes, thinking that he must have needed the rest desperately and she didn't want to wake him. There was work to be done, certainly, but nothing he had to handle immediately.

She went to his desk and picked up the letter from Davenport. Plenty of times in the past, she'd been able to solve problems before they'd ever gotten to Trey. It had been a point of pride with her, almost a game, like "Beat the Clock." She hadn't beaten the clock this time, but maybe there was still something she could do to help.

She slipped out of his office, locking the door behind her so no one would walk in on him. She had to do something. Only one idea occurred to her and, as preposterous as it was, it kept drumming in her brain so that she couldn't ignore it. With a pounding heart, she opened her phone file to ''D'' and dialed Davenport's office.

His secretary answered.

''This is Jane Miller from Breckenridge Construction. I'd like to speak with Mr. Davenport, please.'' Jane moved the phone to her other ear, noticing her palms were slick with nervous perspiration.

''Jane?'' the secretary responded with startling enthusiasm. ''Is that really you? This is Debbie Lancaster. We used to work at Skyron together.''

Jane's shoulders relaxed fractionally. A friendly voice. She hadn't been prepared for that. ''Debbie. Of course I remember you. How are you?''

''Fabulous, just fabulous. Singleton finally asked me to marry him—you remember Singleton, don't you?—so we're tying the knot in May. Of course, we have to go to Des Moines, because that's where his family's from, but that's okay with me.''

Jane bit down on her lower lip. She wasn't in much of a mood for this kind of girl-talk but if Debbie was Davenport's secretary, she might be able to help Jane figure out what had happened to the contract. ''Congratulations, Debbie,'' she said, mustering as much cheerfulness as she could. ''You must be thrilled.''

''I am, I am. So what about you? You're working at Breckenridge now? Is the company really going under?''

This was exactly the kind of opening Jane needed. "Going under? No! Where on earth did you hear that?"

"Haven't you heard? We had a huge contract with Breckenridge, but my boss found out that the company was going bankrupt and he pulled out. Right on time, as it turns out, because we hear things are really dire there. Sorry to be the one to break it to you." She didn't actually sound sorry at all.

Jane tried to stay calm. "Debbie, do you have any idea where your boss heard that?"

"Sure. One of his golf buddies loaned the company the money and they won't pay him back. He was a shareholder and everything. He thought he was protecting his investment and helping out an old friend, now he's out in the cold. To the tune of fifty-million bucks."

Jane gasped. "Fifty-million? Are you sure he said fifty-million?"

"Fifty-million." She lowered her voice conspiratorially. "And the president of the company doesn't even own any interest in it, did you know that? He's got nothing to lose. That's the part that really got Simon—Simon's my boss—he said that if the guy he's dealing with doesn't have any money in the company, he's sure as hell not going to invest. Those were his words."

Jane frowned. "So you think that's why he pulled out?"

"Sure. Wouldn't you?"

"This golf buddy you're talking about. Is that, by any chance, Philip Rankin?"

"Y-yes. How did you know?"

She tapped her fingernails on the desk. "I need to see your boss. Can you make me an appointment this afternoon?"

A barrier went up. Obviously Debbie wasn't comfortable with the possibility of someone else knowing more about this soap opera than she did. "You want to see Simon?"

Jane thought quickly and decided there was only one sure way to get Debbie's help with this. "You won't believe what's going on here."

"Ooh—what?" She was giddy again.

"Philip Rankin was once in love with—" She paused dramatically, mentally counting to three. "I can't go into this on the phone. I really have to talk to your—to Simon first, before I go spewing all sorts of hot gossip…" She let it dangle, hoping Debbie would pick up the bait.

She did. "Well, wait a minute, let me see." There was a moment of quiet in which Jane heard Debbie rifling through papers. "Do you think you can get here within half an hour?"

Jane stood up. "I'm on my way."

"I'll put you down for three. He's only got fifteen minutes."

"That's enough." She could barely contain her excitement. "I'll be right over."

As she drove to Davenport's office, Jane went through a mental checklist to make sure she hadn't forgotten any important details before she'd left. She'd run off three more copies of the Davenport contract, and called Dick Monroe to confirm that she was now the signatory on such matters. She'd left a note for Trey, telling him to wait for her and take no action on the Davenport matter until he'd heard from her. She'd also made copies of the loan papers from Rankin, showing the actual amount due, just in case she actually needed such things to prove her case.

The only thing she hadn't done was come up with a brilliant game plan for when she met with Davenport. She'd never met him before, and had no idea what sort of person he was. All she could do was hope and pray he was the kind of man who would listen to logic and who could be persuaded by honest intentions. In her mind she rehearsed all the ways in which Breckenridge was the best company for the job. She had a little more trouble figuring out a way to hint at the fact that Rankin might have a personal agenda without actually slinging mud.

It wasn't going to be easy.

When she got to the office, Debbie rushed out from behind her desk, nearly hanging herself with her telephone headset in the process, to give Jane a big hug. As soon as she saw the ring on Jane's finger, she asked, "Did you get married?"

It was one of many times in her life that Jane would have liked to have had a cream pie in hand. "You sound surprised," she answered coolly.

"I am," Debbie blustered on. "Who did you marry?"

Jane gritted her teeth and tried to muster some decorum. "Gosh, I thought I told you when we spoke earlier. My husband is Trey Breckenridge." Debbie looked at her blankly. "The president of Brecken-ridge Construction."

That did it. Debbie's jaw dropped. "The president of the company! No wonder you want to see Simon about saving that contract." She smiled approvingly. "I like to see a girl standing up for her man."

She felt her face grow warm. "I want to save the contract because your boss unfortunately got his facts wrong. Breckenridge can do the best job for him, and he already agreed to give us the job." It was difficult to keep her voice from sounding too chilly. "And because a lot of people are going to be out of work if he doesn't honor his commitment."

Debbie smiled guilelessly. "All of that makes sense to me, but I still think it's cool that you're going to bat for your guy. Good luck."

"Thanks." Jane was about to sit down when Simon Davenport's office door creaked open.

Simon Davenport glanced at her, then at the empty waiting room and then at Debbie.

"This is your three o'clock appointment," Debbie said.

Jane gave a cool smile and extended her hand. "Jane. Jane Miller Breckenridge." She noticed his palm was cold and damp and for a moment she nearly backed down.

"Breckenridge, eh? Come in," he said, ushering her in. He directed her to the chair opposite his mas-sive desk, and closed the door behind him.

Jane sat and waited patiently for him to do the same. "I'm here to see you about the contract you have with Breckenridge Construction."

"We dissolved that contract," he said, pulling a handkerchief out of his pocket to mop his forehead.

"I was hoping you'd reconsider that," Jane said, eyeing him steadily. "Would you like me to go into the reasons why?"

He leaned back in his chair and regarded her. "I'm a reasonable man. I'm always willing to consider both sides of an issue before doing anything hasty."

She nodded slowly. "I can certainly appreciate that." For a moment, she had to keep from smiling. This was almost fun. It was completely unlike anything she'd ever done, or even could have imagined herself doing, but here she was, doing it.

And he was actually listening.

"I'll get right to the point," Jane said, noticing what appeared to be a tiny smile on the man's face as she did. "I'm here to correct an injustice."

He screwed his eyebrows up. "What injustice is that?"

"The injustice of Davenport Hotels against Breckenridge Construction." She took a breath and clenched her hands into fists in her lap. "Although we've both been victimized by a third party, a Mr. Rankin."

He nodded. "Go on."

"When you reneged on our contract, I believe you did so under a gross misunderstanding about our company's stability. I'm here today to get the contracts signed so we can go on with our business as planned." She hesitated. "Breckenridge Construction always honors its responsibilities and promises and we expect the same from others." She realized she sounded like someone in a Frank Capra movie, but she meant every word she said and, amazingly, Simon Davenport seemed to appreciate that.

He raised an eyebrow and laced his fingers before him. "You definitely have my attention."

She went on to explain the misinformation he'd gotten from Rankin, the fact that she could prove it, and, most importantly, she described Trey's commitment to the company and to the Davenport Hotel job. As she spoke, Simon Davenport fidgeted with his handkerchief before him, occasionally nodding or making a noise to indicate interest. By the time she had finished what she thought was a darn good pitch, Davenport had agreed to sign the contracts, Debbie had witnessed, and the accounting department had cut the check that would save Breckenridge Construction and Trey.

And would end Jane's marriage.

Trey slammed the telephone receiver down. "Damn it. No one knows where she is."

"This," Terrence said to Trey, "is exactly why I got out of the business."

"This is a very unusual circumstance," Trey said, leafing through the employee list looking for someone he hadn't yet asked about Jane.

"No, son, it's not," the older man said tiredly. "In this business, there's always something nipping at your heels. This time it was the call on the loan, and a contract that fell through. Next time it will be an accident with scaffolding somewhere, or a fire on site."

It was true. There did always seem to be something out there, threatening the company's security and his peace of mind. "It's the nature of the business," he said aloud, running his pen down the list of telephone extensions.

"Oh, yes. Yes, it is. I spent years swinging from one crisis to another until finally my doctor said if I didn't stop I was going to kill myself."

Trey stopped and looked up. "I didn't know the doctor said that to you."

Terrence shrugged. "You and I were at odds. If I'd told you, it would have been admitting a weakness, and I wasn't about to do that. Not back then."

"So why now?"

"Because now I've gained the distance and, dare I say, the wisdom to realize that those games don't pay off. None of this pays off." He leaned toward the desk, his watery-blue eyes penetrating Trey's. "Don't make the same mistakes I did. Don't wait until you're an old man before you stop the madness and enjoy your life."

A tremor shook through Trey's chest. It was gone in an instant, but it left Trey unsettled. "I'm not the same as you," he said, sounding a little like a defensive child.

"No, you're not. But in your way you burn as much energy here as I ever did." He leaned back in his chair. "Did you know that when you were in school, they sent me notes of concern about your grades?"

"My grades were almost perfect."

"Exactly. The psychologist at Carlisle said she

was concerned that you were diving into your studies as a way of making up for loneliness and abandonment." He quirked his mouth and gave an embarrassed shrug. "At the time I thought it was the biggest crock I'd ever heard. The boy applies himself to his studies and the school calls it psychological distress." He glanced down. "If I'd done something about it then, I might have saved you so much pain."

Trey tried to swallow the lump in his throat. "Dad, I was just a good student. There was no hidden psychology behind it." His voice didn't have the conviction it could have.

"Don't make the same mistakes I made," Terrence said again, with a new vehemence. "Your wife loves you. You could have a wonderful life together, or you could both burn yourselves out here with nothing to show for it in forty years except regret and a medicine cabinet full of heart pills."

The office was in an uproar by the time Jane got back. Word had quickly spread that there was something urgent happening in the president's office and that Jane was nowhere to be found.

When she finally walked in, Trey wasn't sure whether to kiss her or strangle her. First he had to find out where she'd gone.

"I went to see Davenport," she said, closing the office door.

"You what?"

"Then I went to the bank to deposit the money." He was stupefied. "The money?"

She nodded and opened her soft leather briefcase.

"The deal's back on. Here are the ratified contracts." She dropped the heavy documents on his desk.

Trey swallowed and stared at Jane in awe. "Is this a dream? Or have I actually died?"

She laughed. "Neither." She sat heavily in the chair opposite him. "We're back where we thought we were a few weeks ago. Everything should be okay now, but I'm going to let you take care of Rankin."

His heart pounded. Never before had he been so filled with admiration for any human being. "How did you do it?"

The old Trey would have felt like she'd stolen his thunder. After all, he'd had a plan himself. But he just couldn't muster anything other than sheer awe at the fact that she'd taken matters into her own hands and won.

He couldn't wait to hear her story.

She was characteristically modest. "It was luck, Trey. I went there, hoping to convince him to do what was right. Already I can see how naive that was. I almost can't believe I did it. But while I was there, things just...well, all the conditions were right. You were right, Rankin had misled him. Once he realized that Breckenridge was stable and reliable, he didn't have any trouble signing the contracts."

His heart was full, but most of the joy he felt was in his pride in her, not from the deal. "I'm running out of words to thank you."

She shook her head. "Don't bother. Believe me, I was no hero. We were just lucky." She sighed and glanced at her hands in her lap. "I'll call Dick and get him to...to start divorce proceedings." She looked at him uncertainly, wondering if it had sounded as much like a question to him as it had to her.

"Oh." A pang shot through his chest. *Your wife loves you.* "I'd almost forgotten about that. For all the anxiety of getting married, it ended up being pretty painless, all in all, didn't it?" He thought of the afternoon they'd just spent together. Did that change things? It felt like it did. No matter what the reason for their marriage, it didn't seem right to initiate a divorce now that they'd just gotten together.

"So far," she said, in a weak voice. She seemed exhausted. He imagined her working under this kind of strain for the next forty years, and felt another pang. Maybe she wanted out of the situation. Maybe she needed out.

As efficient as she was, surely she wouldn't have mentioned the divorce without elaboration if she thought there was anything to elaborate. He cleared his throat. "I guess I should have Monroe write up something for Rankin to sign too, clearing the debt."

She stood up. "I'll call and tell him." Suddenly he noticed her eyes were reddened.

He didn't want to do this anymore.

"Jane," he started, consciously trying to let go of the tight emotional restrictions he held on to.

She glanced up at him quickly. "Yes?"

He drew back, setting the controls back in place. "Why don't you go home and get some rest. You look like you could use it. I'll take care of everything here."

She took a deep, shuddering breath, then nodded.

"All right. I'll go pack my things at the condo and go back to the apartment." She stopped and looked down at her hand. "Oh, you'll need these back too." She started to try and pull both rings off her ring finger but he tried to stop her.

"You don't have to do that yet." He didn't want her to do that. Was he crazy? Had the strain actually gotten to him? At that moment, he thought he could throw it all away and run off with her. But he couldn't. He couldn't. "I'll send the stuff over later. You just take it easy now." He jotted a note on his ink blotter to call Monroe and put the rings in his coat pocket.

"Thanks. I will." She started walking toward the door, then stopped and turned back. "Trey."

"Mmm?" He looked up from his writing.

"I'll be submitting my resignation as well."

His heart gave a solid bang. "You're quitting?"

"I have to." She looked pained.

"Why?"

"Because I love you," she blurted out. For just a moment she hesitated, looking uncertain. Then she smiled. It was a wide, genuine, beautiful smile. "Wow. I never thought I'd say it." She laughed. "It wasn't even that hard." She looked at him evenly. "Trey, I've been in love with you for so long I couldn't even tell you when it began. I would do anything for you except deceive myself by continuing to pretend."

Trey's chest tightened. His throat tightened. He was speechless, but he had to say something. With some effort, he said, "I had no idea, Jane."

"Of course you didn't." She threw her hands in the air. "I never would have had the nerve to tell you if it weren't for everything we've been through these past few weeks. You gave me confidence in myself and for that I'll always be grateful," tears formed in her eyes, "but I can't lie to myself or you by staying here and pretending I don't feel this way."

He swallowed, then swallowed again. He was on a cliff, about to topple over. The silence stretched out as he looked around the office, searching for he-didn't-know-what. Answers? Signs? Maybe he was just memorizing it for posterity. "What will you do next?" he heard himself ask.

"I don't know. There have been offers over the years, maybe I'll follow up on some of them."

He frowned. Jealousy stung like an arrow to the heart. There had been offers? People had been trying to steal Jane from him? The idea was infuriating. Worse, he'd been so blind he hadn't had a clue. "How..." He stopped. Words failed him. "I have another idea."

Everything went still.

He got up and walked across the room to her. He stopped in front of her, put his hands on her shoulders, and looked deeply into her eyes. "How would you like to try something completely different?"

"What do you mean?" she whispered.

He cocked his head. "I don't know. I'm not sure. But I'm thinking maybe you and I could sell our interest in Breckenridge Construction and form a new partnership. Of some sort."

She smiled up at him, causing his heart to clench in anticipation. "Just what did you have in mind?"

Confidence surged through him. It was the right thing. He knew it. And it felt great. "A new deal. Very big. Very important. Very personal." He reached into his pocket and felt for the large diamond engagement ring. It was still warm from being on her.

She drew in a quick breath. "I'm open to new opportunities."

"Even personal ones?"

"Especially personal ones."

Holding her gaze with his own, he knelt before her and took her hand in his. He slowly slid the ring onto her finger. "It's come to my attention that…" He laughed. "That I'm pretty madly in love with you and I really do want to spend the rest of my life with you. Well, really, I have to, so I was thinking…maybe…" This wasn't nearly as easy as he would have thought it would be. He felt his face go red and he shrugged. "Help me out here."

She shook her head, but her whole face was alight with happiness. "Nope. This is one thing you're going to have to do all by yourself."

"Okay. Okay." He sobered himself and looked into her eyes again, touching the ring for an instant to make sure it was on right. "Jane, will you marry me?"

She didn't hesitate. "Yes."

"I'll just hold on to this other ring for a little longer. The next time I put it on, it's staying on."

"It nearly did this time," she said, smiling through her tears.

He stood up, happier than he'd ever imagined feeling in his life. "Tell me, have you ever thought about spending Christmas in France?"

She smiled broadly. "Funny enough, I'm thinking about it right now…"

Epilogue

"To the bride and groom." Terrence raised his glass high. "To my son, Trey, and to Jane, his wife."

A murmur of French voices said, "Jane and Trey" and glasses clinked merrily in the intimate little Provençal bistro. Everyone there knew and loved Terrence, and they had come out in droves to help celebrate his son's wedding.

Jane tasted the yeasty, cold champagne and turned to her husband. "I'm not sure I should have more than just a sip."

Trey set her glass on the table for her. "Didn't the doctor say it was all right to have one glass today?" he asked, concern creasing his brow.

"The doctor said it was all right." She put a hand to her still-flat belly. "But I want to take extra care of your son."

"That's why I love you." He leaned over and

kissed her cheek. "But don't forget the sonogram wasn't that clear. This might be your daughter we're talking about. Or twins."

"Don't say it," she groaned, good naturedly. "One thing at a time, please."

A chic, older woman named Annabelle, a good friend of Terrence's, came up to them. "Pardon," she said, laying a hand on each of their shoulders. "Terrence told me about ze beautiful engagement ring. I must have a look at it."

Jane laughed and held up her left hand, so Annabelle could see the pink diamond engagement ring that had once represented an impossible dream and which now represented a beautiful reality.

Annabelle gasped. "It is beautiful. Oh, *c'est magnifique.*" She touched it with her finger, then touched the pale gold and garnet wedding ring and raised an eyebrow to Trey. "And zis must be ze ring that was once your mother's?"

"That's it," he said. "She wanted me to give it to my wife someday. I never thought that day would come." He looked at Jane. "Thank God I was wrong."

"Another toast," Terrence called from across the room. The voices quieted and everyone looked to him.

"Some of you might not know this, but Terrence and Jane have just bought the old vineyard that borders my farm." He raised his glass. "Here's to their success. May your vines always bear fruit, and your harvests always be bountiful."

The glasses clanked again and the guests roared

back to life, laughing and drinking and tapping their glasses to Jane and Trey's future.

Trey reached for Jane's hand under the table and leaned close. "Care to dance, Mrs. Breckenridge?"

She frowned and looked around. "There's no music."

"Ah, that's where you're wrong." He stood up and pulled her into his arms. "We hear our own music."

She leaned her cheek against his shoulder and smiled as he tightened his arm around her and started to sway gently. "I hear it now," she said.

Outside the window, the silver bells from the church where they had just renewed their vows rang across the distance.

* * * * *

*Look for the conclusion
to
Elizabeth Harbison's* CINDERELLA BRIDES
*series
next month in Silhouette Romance.*

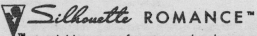

If you enjoyed what you just read,
then we've got an offer you can't resist!

Take 2 bestselling love stories FREE!

Plus get a FREE surprise gift!

Clip this page and mail it to Silhouette Reader Service™

IN U.S.A.	IN CANADA
3010 Walden Ave.	P.O. Box 609
P.O. Box 1867	Fort Erie, Ontario
Buffalo, N.Y. 14240-1867	L2A 5X3

YES! Please send me 2 free Silhouette Romance® novels and my free surprise gift. Then send me 6 brand-new novels every month, which I will receive months before they're available in stores. In the U.S.A., bill me at the bargain price of $2.90 plus 25¢ delivery per book and applicable sales tax, if any*. In Canada, bill me at the bargain price of $3.25 plus 25¢ delivery per book and applicable taxes**. That's the complete price and a savings of over 10% off the cover prices—what a great deal! I understand that accepting the 2 free books and gift places me under no obligation ever to buy any books. I can always return a shipment and cancel at any time. Even if I never buy another book from Silhouette, the 2 free books and gift are mine to keep forever. So why not take us up on our invitation. You'll be glad you did!

215 SEN CNE7
315 SEN CNE9

Name	(PLEASE PRINT)	
Address	Apt.#	
City	State/Prov.	Zip/Postal Code

* Terms and prices subject to change without notice. Sales tax applicable in N.Y.
** Canadian residents will be charged applicable provincial taxes and GST.
   All orders subject to approval. Offer limited to one per household.
   ® are registered trademarks of Harlequin Enterprises Limited.

SROM99   ©1998 Harlequin Enterprises Limited

Silhouette ROMANCE™

One little...two little...three little...BABIES!

What are three confirmed bachelor brothers to do when they suddenly become guardians to triplets?

Find out in bestselling author
Susan Meier's new trilogy

THE BABY BEQUEST—On sale in January 2000
Evan Brewster needed baby lessons fast! And surprisingly, his father's former assistant seemed to have the perfect knack with the baby brood—and with Evan's heart....

BRINGING UP BABIES—On sale in February 2000
Chas Brewster was desperate to hire a nanny, but what was he to do when he wanted Lily's involvement to become much more personal?

OH, BABIES!—On sale in March 2000
Grant Brewster was known for his control—at least until Kristen sneaked her way into his life. Suddenly the all-so-cool bachelor was getting hot and bothered—and enjoying it!

Available at your favorite retail outlet...only from
SILHOUETTE ROMANCE®

Silhouette®
Where love comes alive™

Visit us at www.romance.net   SRBBB

**Start celebrating Silhouette's 20th anniversary
with these 4 special titles by
New York Times bestselling authors**

*Fire and Rain**
by Elizabeth Lowell

King of the Castle
by Heather Graham Pozzessere

*State Secrets**
by Linda Lael Miller

*Paint Me Rainbows**
by Fern Michaels

On sale in December 1999

Available at your favorite retail outlet
**Also available on audio from Brilliance.*

Silhouette®
Where love comes alive™

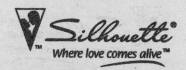